"Let me get this straight," Taylor said. *"You want me—your wife—to pretend to be your wife?"*

"Yes. Pretend to be my loving, affectionate, definitely-not-estranged wife."

"I'm a waitress, Jake. Not an actress."

"I know it will be a challenge, but I'll make it worth your while. All I need you to do is come back to Montana with me. You'll have a free place to stay and all the food you can eat for a week."

"Free room and board, Jake? For your wife? How generous."

"Taylor…"

"Getting back together is not a smart idea."

"It's only for a week. We can tolerate each other that long, can't we?"

Unfortunately, Taylor realized, it wasn't just an issue of tolerating each other. They also had to keep their hands to themselves.

And with the chemistry between them still as strong as ever, it was going to be a challenge.

A *big* challenge.

Dear Reader,

Unforgettable Bride, by bestselling author Annette Broadrick, is May's VIRGIN BRIDES selection, *and* the much-requested spin-off to her DAUGHTERS OF TEXAS series. Rough, gruff rodeo star Bobby Metcalf agreed to a quickie marriage—sans honeymoon!—with virginal Casey Carmichael. But four years later, he's still a married man—one intent on being a husband to Casey in every sense....

Fabulous author Arlene James offers the month's FABULOUS FATHERS title, *Falling for a Father of Four.* Orren Ellis was a single dad to a brood of four, so hiring sweet Mattie Kincaid seemed the perfect solution. Until he found himself falling for this woman he could never have.... Stella Bagwell introduces the next generation of her bestselling TWINS ON THE DOORSTEP series. In *The Rancher's Blessed Event,* an ornery bronc rider must open his heart both to the woman who'd betrayed him...and her child yet to be born.

Who can resist a sexy, stubborn cowboy—particularly when he's your husband? Well, Taylor Cassidy tries in Anne Ha's *Long, Tall Temporary Husband.* But will she succeed? And Sharon De Vita's irresistible trio, LULLABIES AND LOVE, continues with *Baby with a Badge,* where a bachelor cop finds a baby in his patrol car...and himself in desperate need of a woman's touch! Finally, new author C.J. Hill makes her commanding debut with a title that sums it up best: *Baby Dreams and Wedding Schemes.*

Romance has everything you need from new beginnings to tried-and-true favorites. Enjoy each and every novel this month, and every month!

Warm Regards!

Joan Marlow Golan

Joan Marlow Golan
Senior Editor, Silhouette Romance

Please address questions and book requests to:
Silhouette Reader Service
U.S.: 3010 Walden Ave., P.O. Box 1325, Buffalo, NY 14269
Canadian: P.O. Box 609, Fort Erie, Ont. L2A 5X3

LONG, TALL TEMPORARY HUSBAND

Anne Ha

Silhouette

ROMANCE™

Published by Silhouette Books

America's Publisher of Contemporary Romance

To both of our families with much love

 SILHOUETTE BOOKS

ISBN 0-373-19297-5

LONG, TALL TEMPORARY HUSBAND

Copyright © 1998 by Anne Ha and Joe Thoron

Books by Anne Ha

Silhouette Romance

Husband Next Door #1208
Her Forgotten Husband #1232
Long, Tall Temporary Husband #1297

ANNE HA

is really the award-winning husband/wife writing team of Anne Ha and Joe Thoron. The couple met at Amherst College, where they both majored in English and Women's Studies—a great preparation for writing romance novels.

Anne and Joe have always loved books and particularly enjoy reading aloud to each other. They also love to garden on warm summer days, to travel and to meet all different kinds of people. They can't imagine a world without "The X-Files," ice cream and naughty cats.

You can write to them at P.O. Box 225, Amherst, MA 01004-0225.

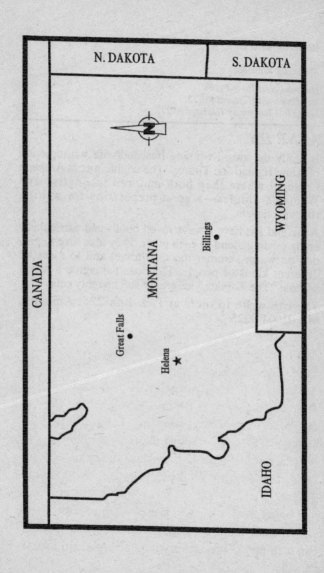

Prologue

Taylor tossed her leather suitcase onto the bed, yanked open the zippers and threw back the top. "I hate you, Jake! And I hate this godforsaken ranch!"

She stalked to the dresser and pulled out a drawer. She carried it to the bed and upended it over the suitcase. Nightgowns and lingerie tumbled out.

Dropping the empty drawer onto the bedspread, she stormed back over to the dresser for another drawer. Socks, leggings, cotton tank tops. It all went into the suitcase. The drawer joined the other on the bed.

Jake stood behind her, tension filling his body, a look of disgust on his face. "You're a spoiled brat, Taylor."

T-shirts, jeans, blouses, slacks. "Go to hell!"

"And a wimp. Go ahead, run home to your parents. I'm sure they'll make everything all right. No reason they should stop babying you just because you're an adult.''

She threw open the closet door. Grabbing a few dresses, she crammed them into the suitcase, hangers and all.

The suitcase was a disaster. Sleeves and hems stuck out over the edge. Everything lay in a crumpled mess, but Taylor didn't care.

She darted into the bathroom, grabbed her toiletry kit from a drawer in the vanity and jammed handfuls of cosmetics into it. Her eye pencil snapped going into the kit. She hurled the pieces into the trash can.

Jake loomed in the doorway. "One month, Taylor. You lasted one month." His voice dripped scorn. "Even my mother lasted longer than that."

She snatched up the toiletry kit and barreled past him into the bedroom. "It wasn't one month," she muttered. "It was five weeks. Five of the most horrible weeks of my—"

"Privileged, coddled, self-absorbed life."

She dropped the toiletry kit onto the pile of rumpled clothes and pounded on the pile with her fists until it was compact enough to get the top closed. The zipper stuck halfway, blocked by a T-shirt. Giving a fluent curse, she ripped the offending item out of the way, tossed it to the ground and finished with the zipper.

She whirled to face him. "You know, if you'd ever stopped working long enough to have a conversation with me, we might have had a chance."

"We talked plenty."

"Yeah, right. You talked. *Taylor, I need you. Taylor. Oh, God, Taylor. I can't resist you, Taylor...*" She glared at him. "It was always when we were— when we were—"

"Having sex? Well, what do you expect? Our whole relationship is based on physical attraction. Aside from that we have nothing in common." He laughed bitterly. "I should have known you were off limits the moment I saw you in that three-hundred-dollar swimsuit. How could a rich city slicker like you ever be happy in Montana?"

Taylor slung her purse over her shoulder, grabbed the heavy suitcase and marched out the door. She dragged it to the top of the stairs and tossed it down. It fell end over end, landing with a thud on the floor-boards below.

She descended the steps, picked it up and heaved it onto the porch.

Jake's pickup was parked outside, the keys on the dash as usual. She lurched over to it, dumped her suitcase in the back and got in. "Go muck out some stalls, Jake."

Anger radiated from him, but he didn't move to stop her. "Something you've never done."

"I married you, Jake, not your ranch."

"And you thought I'd do nothing but pamper you? You're a fool."

Taylor fired up the truck. Through the open window she said, "Find another wife, Jake. Some empty-headed country girl who's never been to the big bad city. She'll be happy here. You can shovel horse manure together.''

"Don't come back, Taylor. You don't belong here.''

She fixed him with her most withering glare. "Believe me, Jake. Nothing could ever convince me to set foot on this ranch again.''

Taylor threw the truck into gear and peeled out in a cloud of dust.

She got fifty yards away before she jammed on the brakes, made a reckless three-point turn and sped back to the house. She pulled up in front of Jake, ripped the wedding set from her finger and threw both rings into the dirt at his feet. Then, without a word, she stomped on the gas and roared down the drive.

Back at the house, Jake stared after her. He watched his truck disappear around the bend. Slowly the dust settled until all traces of his wife's flight had vanished.

She was gone.

Gone. As if she'd never been here. As if the past five weeks were nothing but a childish fantasy, a naive dream. She was gone, and good riddance.

He bent down and lifted her rings off the ground. He blew the dirt off them, rubbed them clean. They were still warm with the heat of her body, and as he slipped them into his pocket an ache settled deep in his chest.

Good riddance? Who was he trying to kid? Depression closed over him. He'd thought they had a future together. He'd lost his heart to her and she'd behaved exactly as he'd feared, abandoning him along with her discarded rings.

With a last look at the empty drive, he turned and headed for the barn. He would lose himself in work, and eventually he would forget her.

Chapter One

Five months later

"Excuse me, Miss, but this toast is burned. And I clearly asked for real half-and-half with my coffee, not this nondairy junk."

Taylor stared down at the annoying customer seated at table fifteen, wishing he would just disappear. Every Saturday morning he came to the Pancake Hut for breakfast, and every Saturday morning he found something wrong with his food—which meant she had to take it back to the kitchen.

The cook—her boss—hated it when she took an order back. He usually got mad and purposely messed up her next several orders.

That had the same result every time. Lower tips.

Taylor needed those tips. Desperately. She lived

from paycheck to paycheck, barely managing to keep a roof over her head and make payments on the debts she'd racked up several months ago. So instead of telling Mr. Annoying where he could put his toast— which was what she would have done a few months ago—she gritted her teeth and counted to ten.

He waved to his side order plate. "What are you gonna do about my toast? I'm hungry and I don't got all day."

She reached for the toast. The slices were a light golden brown, not burned at all. It figured. "I'm very sorry, sir. I'll replace this as quickly as I can." If she timed it right, she could do it herself while the cook was busy at the grill. If he didn't see her she'd be all right.

The customer huffed, then gave her a grudging nod. "What about my cream?"

"We don't have any, but I could bring some milk. Would that do?"

"Well, be quick about it."

Fighting the urge to bop the man on the head, Taylor turned away from the table.

That was when she saw him. Jake. Standing at the entrance to the coffee shop, gorgeous and rugged in faded jeans and a thick shearling coat.

In the space of an instant, Taylor's world shifted sideways. She felt as if her stomach had plummeted to the ground. Her whole body tingled with shock.

Five months, she thought. It had been five long, challenging months since she'd seen him, yet it might have been only yesterday. He was so much the same, so familiar with that long, lean rancher's body and thick dark hair.

How many times this fall had she imagined being with him again? Imagined what it would feel like to be in his arms again, warm and comforted instead of alone in a cold, impersonal city?

Everything about him had haunted her. His seductive brown eyes, the masculine grace of his movements, the warm scent of his skin. She remembered the first day they'd met, on vacation last summer. The sensations came back to her: hot sun on her skin, powder-soft sand underfoot. The scent of suntan lotion. And Jake, sitting there on the beach in Mexico, propped up on his elbows, watching her walk by. She'd felt an intense attraction the moment her gaze had locked onto his chiseled features and dark, wind-tousled hair. And when their eyes had met, she'd felt the most heady response.

It had been a magical week, full of champagne and music and moonlit dancing. They'd eloped before the trip was over, each of them absolutely confident they'd found their life partner.

But then he'd brought her home to the Cassidy Ranch—and everything had fallen apart. Within days she'd felt the change in him. The subtle withdrawal. She'd married him for his passion, for his joy in life, but once on the ranch he'd settled into a pattern of nonstop twelve-hour days and left her to her own devices. Their physical attraction had been strong, but not strong enough to bridge the growing gulf between them.

She'd tried to ignore it. But the feeling of abandonment she'd experienced was all too familiar. Her mother and father had always valued their work and their social lives more than her. She'd thought Jake would be different, that he would value her more, but he didn't.

Their marriage was an impulsive mistake. Though it had started in a passionate whirlwind, it crashed and burned in barely a month.

She watched Jake now as he scanned the busy restaurant, looking for her, she knew. Nothing else would have brought him to Boston, to this dingy little dive in a bad part of town.

And the only reason he'd be looking for her was to initiate their divorce. A sick feeling settled in her stomach. She'd known this day would come, had tried to tell herself it was what she wanted. To be free of him. But that didn't explain her reaction, her sudden flash of despair.

Finally Jake's deep brown eyes locked onto hers, steady, assessing. Feeling like a deer caught in the headlights of a car, she stared back at him, frozen and vulnerable. Even her mind seemed frozen, stuck on that one awful thought. *Divorce.*

Jake crossed the room in a few easy strides, his gaze never leaving hers, his expression unreadable.

"Hello, Taylor."

That voice. Low, rough, whiskey-soft. Seductive even now, when he'd only tracked her down to say their marriage was over.

She wasn't ready for this confrontation. Wasn't

ready to hear that Jake had found someone else, someone who was selfless and caring, mature and responsible. All the things Taylor hadn't been.

But she forced herself to stand firm. "Hello, Jake," she said. Her voice was cool, remote, as if she felt nothing, no anxiety, no pain.

His eyes narrowed almost imperceptibly. Taylor waited for him to say something, but he seemed content to stand there taking in her pink polyester blouse and skirt and frilly white Pancake Hut apron.

Mr. Annoying on fifteen broke the moment. "Hey, Miss! Are you going to get my toast or not?"

She'd forgotten she still held the plate. She gave him her best waitressing smile. "Just a minute," she said as cheerfully as she could. Then she addressed Jake. "Whatever you're here for, I don't have time."

"We need to talk."

"Not right now, we don't." She wondered whether he'd brought the divorce papers with him. Would he whip them out and demand she sign on the dotted line? Would he offer her money? Or would they have to go through a long legal battle she couldn't afford to fight?

"It's important."

Like it or not, her marriage had blown up in her face; the only graceful thing to do was to accept it like a lady. But she didn't feel graceful, and she didn't feel like a lady. She felt like a tired waitress without enough money and way too much loneliness. "Look," she said, "you've already lost me my tip from this guy, and I'm not in the mood."

"I'll pay you the difference."

"Forget it, Jake." She didn't want a dime of his money. She was going to support herself, and prove to herself, her parents and Jake that she wasn't a total loser.

Her mind flashed back over the past five months. When she'd first returned to Boston her need to forget Jake had made her wild and reckless. She'd spent money like crazy, blowing through her father's generous allowance in only six days. Her father had given her more, on the condition she shape up, become an adult, start taking life more seriously. She hadn't. Instead she'd dealt with the pain of her failed marriage the only way she knew how: by buying everything in sight.

Her mother had given her more money, but had said that was it until she got her life together. Taylor hadn't believed her. Her parents had always thrown money at her instead of love; why would anything be different this time?

But it was. Her parents had cut her off. They'd offered her a place to stay and food to eat but only on the condition that she take a paper-pushing, closely supervised job in the personnel department at her father's company.

Chafing at their control like a petulant child, Taylor had thrown it back in their faces. She'd moved in with a friend that afternoon. But her credit cards were tapped out, and none of the stylish jobs she applied for worked out. In the end, she couldn't keep up with her friends' glamorous life-styles, and they blew her off.

She'd had no money, no job, no friends, no place to live. She'd thrown it all away. She'd been a fool, and pride prevented her from accepting her parents' new tough-love brand of assistance.

Finally she'd tried in earnest to get a job, and ended up a week later at the Pancake Hut. She'd done more growing up in that one week, and in the months of backbreaking restaurant work that followed, than she had in her entire life. With newfound grit and determination, she'd started to get her life back together.

And she'd keep doing it—alone.

Taylor pointed into the kitchen where her boss, Sleazy Steve, glared at her over the grill. "Do you see that man back there? If I'm more than thirty seconds late to pick up a plate he burns my next two orders. So I don't really care what you have to talk to me about. It's not more important than my job."

Jake fixed his gaze on her, unblinking. "You don't know that." His tone was even, calm. Not argumentative, but still it raised Taylor's hackles.

Like herself, Jake could be an incredibly stubborn person. "You might not believe it, Jake, but nothing is more important than my job. Nothing."

Not even you. Not even my husband. The words remained unspoken, but she knew they both heard them echo through the restaurant.

Five months and one week ago she never would have even thought those words. Five months and one week ago her husband had been the most important thing in her life. But she hadn't been the most important thing in his. Not by a long shot.

"I'm not going to leave," Jake said.

"Fine," Taylor returned. "You can wait all day for me if you want. Just don't do it in the aisle."

That brought a hint of a smile to his lips. "Where's your section?"

"Over there." She pointed. "But don't you dare..." She trailed off as Jake sauntered over to the only vacant booth in her section. He slipped out of his shearling coat and sat down.

Taylor took a deep breath and counted to ten. By seven she'd calmed down, and when she hit ten she knew how she'd handle the situation. The moment Jake had sat down he'd become a customer. Nothing more, nothing less.

And she'd learned how to deal with customers.

She ducked into the kitchen to make fresh toast for the man on fifteen, then took a menu to Jake. She slid it onto the table. "Coffee?"

He met her eyes. "Taylor..."

A lot of her customers liked to call her by her first name. It was written on a little plastic tag pinned to her blouse. But no one said it in that rough, sexy way, like a lion trying to growl but ending up purring. "Cream or sugar?" she asked brightly.

She knew how he took his coffee. Black and strong.

"Neither."

Turning on her heel, Taylor checked on her other customers, then took Jake his coffee.

He hadn't touched the menu, but she pulled out her order pad anyway. "What do you want?"

Jake took a sip of his coffee. "I need fifteen minutes of your time. Maybe half an hour."

Enough time to sign the papers, she guessed. "What do you want that's on the menu? I recommend the pancakes." After all, this was the Pancake Hut.

"Hear me out, Taylor."

"Okay, pancakes it is. Short or tall?"

"Tall. Come on. For old times' sake."

"Real or fake?"

"Excuse me?"

"Syrup. Real or fake?"

"Real."

She gave him a bright smile. "Hash browns, bacon and toast with that?"

"You're just going to ignore me, aren't you?"

"Orange juice?"

He sighed. "Sure, Taylor. Bring me whatever you want. But I'm not going away until we talk."

Another smile. "I'll be right back with your juice." She fled for the kitchen.

One of the other waitresses stood at the service counter refilling the coffeemaker. Candy was a bleach-blonde in her late thirties who chewed gum incessantly. She pointed at Jake with her chin. "Who's the dish?"

This wasn't what she needed. Taylor filled a glass of orange juice and tried for an offhand tone. "Him? Just someone I used to know."

"He's cute." Candy craned her head to see across the room. "Is the O.J. for him? I'll take it over."

Candy plucked the glass from her startled fingers and swished away, hips swinging.

"Order up," Sleazy Steve growled.

Taylor put her mind back on her waitressing, but the next time Candy crossed her path Taylor said, "He's married." She wasn't trying to be possessive—even if she *had* felt a strange spark of jealousy—just warning her co-worker away from disappointment.

"The dish? I didn't see a ring."

"Trust me. He's married."

Candy snapped her gum, her expression changing to a mix of anger and pity. All traces of her interest in Jake were gone. "So it's like that, huh? Probably told you he was leaving her, but never did. And he expects you to pine away for him and jump back into his bed whenever he gets in the mood. The skunk. Want me to go pour hot coffee in his lap?"

Taylor almost laughed. "It's not like that."

"Uh-huh. Right."

"He's married to *me*, Candy."

Candy's jaw dropped. "Excuse me?"

"We're married."

Candy snapped her gum again. "Then why in the world are you living alone and working in this dump? Take him back, girl!"

"I don't think so," she said, shaking her head. "It's too late for that."

Sleazy Steve dropped two plates on the service shelf. "Order up, Candy," he barked.

Candy ignored him. "It's never too late, hon."

"We don't like each other."

"Yeah," Candy said. "Which is why he's staring at you like he wants to have you for breakfast."

He was? Taylor's heart rate sped up at the news but she forced herself to take a deep breath and calm down. Jake wasn't here to try to get her back, and she had to remember that.

The cook banged his spatula on the stainless steel counter. "Order up!"

Candy slowly turned and fixed Sleazy Steve with a scorching glare. She popped her gum. "Go suck an egg, Stevie. This is important."

Taylor wanted to burst out laughing, but she knew she'd get fired if she did. Only Candy, for some incomprehensible reason, could get away with such behavior. "Jake doesn't like me, Candy."

"Huh! What's not to like? You're a total sweetheart."

"Thanks, but Jake—"

"Jake's gonna get an earful," Candy declared.

"Don't," Taylor said, but Candy wasn't listening. She took the plates of food from the service shelf and sashayed off.

Taylor stood glued to the floor as Candy dropped her two plates in front of a couple of customers and approached Jake's booth. She couldn't hear what Candy said, but from the way the woman stood with her hands on her hips, she guessed it wasn't friendly.

A minute later Candy came back over.

"What did he say?" Taylor demanded.

Candy shrugged. "Nothing much. I told him you were a great girl and he'd been a fool to leave you. He told me, very politely, that it was none of my business." She popped her gum. "Not exactly the type to unburden his soul to a total stranger, is he?"

"No." That was an understatement. Jake was a typical cowboy—stoic and silent when it came to matters of the heart. Even when that matter of the heart was a marriage gone bad.

"He wants to talk with you."

"I know."

"He wouldn't tell me what it was about, but it sounds important."

"I'm sure it is, but I'm not interested."

Candy chewed her gum. "Talk to the man, Taylor."

She started to say, "I'm too busy," but Candy cut her off.

"I'll cover your section," the other woman said.

Taylor glanced around the busy restaurant. "Thanks, Candy, but—"

"No buts. The guy's your husband. At least go hear what he has to say."

"Steve's going to kill me if I take an early break."

"I'll handle it."

As if on cue, Sleazy Steve slammed a plate of pancakes down on the service counter. It was Jake's order.

"Take it over," Candy said. "I'll bring you something in a minute. Eggs and toast okay?"

Resigned to her fate, Taylor reached for the order. "Sure, Candy. And thanks. I think."

Jake watched his wife cross the room, a plate of food in her strong, slender hands. He'd always enjoyed watching her—the unconscious rhythm of her steps, the sway of her hips, the way she carried her head high and proud.

She put the plate down in front of him and then, to his surprise, slid onto the opposite bench.

He watched as she settled herself, her back straight against the cushion. She didn't look happy to be there.

"Hello, Taylor," he said.

"Jake."

"Thanks for coming over."

She shrugged. "No problem."

Jake glanced down at his plate, then up at Taylor. He didn't pick up his fork. A lot was riding on the next half hour. The future of the Cassidy Ranch was in his hands, and in hers.

Taylor looked so different from how she had the summer before. Her expression was wary and uncertain, not at all like the composed, self-possessed woman he'd married. She was too thin, and her skin had a pallor to it, instead of the healthy glow of before.

For a moment he felt almost sorry for her. If the past five months had been hard on him, they'd obviously been harder on her. He'd only lost his heart.

She'd lost her whole life-style—the clothes, the fast cars, the parties.

As soon as his mind formed the thought, his pity vanished.

Taylor glared at him from across the table. "How did you find me?"

"I called your father a couple of days ago." He paused, then added, "I didn't know, Taylor." He wondered whether that would make any difference to her. He'd spent the past five months assuming she was living her carefree life in Boston, never imagining the truth.

Hell, he was still her husband. He still had responsibilities toward her that wouldn't end until the divorce papers were signed.

Divorce papers. Despite his dislike of Taylor's behavior on the ranch last summer, despite their differences, the thought of signing divorce papers still left him with a hollow feeling in his gut. Since the day she'd stormed off the ranch, he'd been waiting for the papers to show up in the mail, dreading the moment. But they never had.

After talking to her father, though, he thought he knew the reason. Taylor probably hadn't had the time or the money to find an attorney to file the papers. A nasty job in a dirty restaurant wouldn't leave her a lot of extra money. Certainly not as much spare cash as she'd used to have.

He planned to use that to his advantage.

"Tell me why you're here, Jake."

He took a deep breath. "I need your help." God,

but he hated having to ask her for a favor. He'd much rather have her in *his* debt than the other way around.

"My help?" Was that a note of surprise he detected? Surprise that he would throw away his pride enough to ask her for a favor?

"Yes," he answered. There was nothing for it. He made himself say the words. "I need your help to buy a piece of land."

She blinked. "Jake, I don't exactly have a lot of spare cash right now."

"I don't need your money, Taylor." This was the crux of it. Even if she still had access to her trust fund and her allowance, it wouldn't help him at all. Jake had more than enough cash to buy the land he wanted. He just didn't have...his wife. "I don't need your money," he repeated. "I need you."

I need you. Such a simple phrase, but so devastating to say. All his life he'd done his best to avoid it. And after she'd left he'd sworn he wouldn't ever say those three words to anyone, wouldn't ever let himself feel those emotions. But here he was, saying them to none other than Taylor Cassidy.

She leaned back in her chair, a look of disbelief on her face. She tucked a lock of her hair behind her ear. A rich chocolate brown, it had grown out from the short, stylish cut she'd worn before, now curving just below her jaw.

He liked it. It wasn't so polished and perfect. And he wanted to sink his hands into that extra hair, to feel it sliding through his fingers.

Even now he fought the urge to reach across the

table to feel it, to see if it was still as soft as he remembered. They'd used to be husband and wife, free to touch or caress each other when the mood struck. Now there was a wall between them.

In five months of living alone he'd finally gotten used to not having her around. But being so close to her again threw that all to the wind. He was right back to where he'd been last summer, wanting her so much he couldn't think straight.

Jake took a moment to calm his senses. He had to be rational today. Totally unlike the man who'd fallen for Taylor like a ton of bricks last summer. His future was on the line; he couldn't let his past mess it up.

"You need me to do what?" Taylor asked.

"I need you to be my wife again."

She stared at him long and hard. "Forget it." She started to slide out of the booth.

"Taylor, sit down. It wouldn't be real. I just need you to pretend to be my wife. For a week."

Taylor stayed in her seat. Jake suspected it was because the blond waitress showed up just then with a glass of milk and a plate of eggs and toast, rather than because he'd asked her to.

She picked up her fork. "Let me know when you regain your sanity, okay?"

Jake opened his mouth to explain his predicament, but Taylor held up her hand for silence. He kept his mouth shut while she ate. Jake took a bite of his pancakes. They were surprisingly good, so he ate while he waited for Taylor.

Finally she finished and took a sip of her milk. "I can't tell you how tired I am of breakfast food."

Was she just going to ignore his request? "Taylor…"

She straightened. "Right. Back to business." Shaking her head, she said, "Let me get this straight. You want me—your wife—to pretend to be your wife?"

"Yes. Pretend to be my loving, affectionate, definitely-not-estranged wife."

"I'm a waitress, Jake. Not an actress."

"I know it'll be a challenge, but I'll make it worth your while. I'll pay you."

He'd expected her to jump at the offer, but she didn't. Instead she waved a hand around the Pancake Hut. "I already have a job."

He'd noticed. But even though it was just the kind of work she needed to give her a dose of reality, he didn't like the way her customers leered at her. And he didn't guess she earned much money for her efforts. "What do you make here?"

Taylor hesitated, then named a ridiculously low figure.

"That's all?" He didn't know how she even paid for a place to stay on that kind of money, much less any health insurance. Taylor had some hard lessons to learn, but even Jake didn't think she should be risking her welfare to learn them. "Including tips?"

"Yes, Jake. This place doesn't attract big tippers."

"I'll pay you four times that for a week in Montana."

She ignored him and took another sip of milk.

He wasn't reaching her. She might not make much,

but four times that amount was getting to be some serious cash. Obviously she wanted to play hardball.

Well, so be it. "Your father told me you've got some debts. I'll pay them off, help you make a fresh start. And of course you'll have a free place to stay and all the food you can eat for a week."

"Free room and board, Jake? For your wife? How generous."

Another sip of milk. Jake watched her small pink tongue dart out to dab her lip and felt an unwanted resurgence of desire.

He grimaced unhappily. "Taylor…"

She speared a pancake off his plate and put it on hers. "Getting back together is not a smart idea."

"It's only for a week. We can tolerate each other that long, can't we?"

Unfortunately it wasn't just an issue of tolerating each other. They also had to keep their hands to themselves, too. With the chemistry between them still as strong as ever, it might be a big challenge.

"When exactly do you need me?" Taylor asked.

"Tomorrow."

"Tomorrow?"

"Yeah, tomorrow."

"Kind of short notice, don't you think?"

"The situation came up quickly."

Jake explained about Henry Hankins. Back in Montana, Hankins owned the land adjoining Jake's ranch. He'd leased it to Jake for the last six years, providing some much-needed grazing space. The Cassidy Ranch was doing well—expanding, in fact—and land was hard to come by.

Now Hankins, who normally resided in Dallas, had

decided to liquidate his assets. He wanted to sell, and
Jake was the obvious buyer.

Especially since he was married.

Hankins said two other men had made high offers,
but one of them was divorced and the other was a
freewheeling bachelor. It hurt Hankins's upstanding
heart to think of his land going to a man who couldn't
live with decent values.

And, he said, he adored that "perty little gal" Jake
had married. That was the deciding factor.

Hankins had met Taylor last summer when he'd
gone for a visit. He'd been so taken with her that he
hadn't noticed she was a pampered debutante, totally
unsuited to ranch life. He couldn't wait to see that
"perty little gal" again when he came to close the
deal.

Just a few days ago he'd called Jake to say he'd
set aside some vacation time and planned to bring his
grandchildren to show them Montana. Even though it
was the dead of winter, they'd all have a big old blast.

To Jake it had sounded like a big old nightmare.

"Look," he said to Taylor, "I hate dishonesty as
much as the next guy, but if I lose this land to someone else, I'll have to restructure my whole operation.
I'll probably have to lay off some of my ranch hands.
You remember Reid, right? He and his wife just had
a baby. And then there's Dusty, who sends two-thirds
of her paycheck to her grandmother." He paused,
watching her expression. "But I don't expect you to
do this out of altruism," he continued. "Let's make
it a straightforward business deal. You play the role,
and I'll pay you well, plus take care of your debts."

Still no response. He was getting frustrated, so he

played his final card. "And when the week is over, I'll arrange our divorce. Trouble-free, plenty of alimony."

Taylor tucked her paper napkin under the edge of her empty plate and repositioned her glass of milk. Her movements were precise, almost uncomfortable. She didn't meet his eyes. "So Hankins arrives tomorrow?"

He nodded. He wasn't sure how to read her, but it sounded as if she was actually considering coming to Montana. "With his three grandchildren. Irma's tidying up his cabin as we speak."

At the mention of his housekeeper's name, Taylor's expression grew warm and a little wistful. "How is Irma?"

"She's fine." He shouldn't be surprised that Taylor remembered Irma fondly, when the woman had spoiled her rotten.

He'd never understood why Irma had doted on Taylor so much, fixing all her favorite meals and picking up after her without the slightest complaint. She'd happily acted as the handmaid Taylor expected.

Maybe it was because it had been so long since a woman had lived in the Cassidy ranch house. Thirty-six years, to be exact. Since Jake's mother had left, abandoning her husband and newborn son.

Jake cut off that line of thought. Wallowing in the distant past wouldn't change anything. He focused on the problem at hand. "Well, Taylor, what about it?"

Her wistful expression faded. "Can't you just tell Hankins I went to the city for a week of shopping? He won't miss me."

Jake shook his head. "I know Hankins, and he's

not going to sign off on the land until he sees you again.''

"So you're stuck.''

"Yes, I'm stuck.''

She glanced up at a clock on the wall. "And I need to get back to work.'' She took a long drink, finishing off her milk. She stood.

"Dammit, Taylor.'' He reached out to capture her wrist. "Will you do it?''

She stared down at his hand on her warm skin.

Jake followed her gaze, wishing he hadn't touched her. Currents of electricity rocketed up his arm and spread through his body. He wouldn't have been surprised to see sparks flying from the point of contact.

Five months, he thought, and the effects were still the same.

He released his grasp slowly, trying to make it look casual. As if he'd felt nothing at all.

"Sorry,'' he said under his breath.

Taylor drew herself up. "As I said, I have to get back to work.''

"And the plan?''

"Jake, I swore I'd never set foot on your ranch again.''

"I remember.''

"But I'll think about it. Meet me outside at three o'clock.''

Chapter Two

She didn't really have a choice. Only spite and false pride would have kept her in Boston. Jake's employees needed her help. *Jake* needed her help. She wasn't someone who turned her back on people. Not anymore.

It would be a business deal. A simple, straightforward business deal. An acting assignment. She would leave her heart and her confused emotions out of it. When the week was over she would come back to Boston and make her life better.

Jake's money would buy her enough time to find a better job when she came back. Maybe in a restaurant where the boss didn't verbally assault his workers whenever the mood struck. Maybe in a place where the customers actually knew how to tip.

At three o'clock Jake came back to the restaurant. He led her to a rented sport utility vehicle at the curb.

She gave him directions to her apartment and he pulled into traffic.

"When's our flight?" she asked.

Jake glanced over at her. "You'll help me?"

She shrugged, feigning nonchalance. "Sure."

"Thank you." The words were simple but sincere.

"No problem. I know how much you care about the ranch." More than he had about her, but she didn't want to go there. "It would be petty not to help you just because we don't like each other anymore." She paused, staring out the window at inner city Boston. "Anyway, this arrangement will be good for both of us, so it's not like I'm really doing you a favor."

Jake shook his head. "You're definitely doing me a favor. Especially on such short notice."

"When's our flight?"

"Six a.m. I already bought you a round-trip ticket. And I've got a room reserved for you at one of the airport hotels. We won't have to fight traffic in the morning."

"You were that sure I'd come?"

"No, just desperate."

A few minutes later they pulled up in front of her building. The façade was weathered brick, its windows dirty and cracked. She led Jake up the worn staircase and down the hall to her studio apartment.

He stepped into the single room and looked around. She saw it through his eyes: the peeling institutional green walls, the stains and cigarette burns on the vinyl flooring. The battered dresser and wardrobe, the narrow bed. The forlorn jade plant on the windowsill where it could soak up what little light came down between the apartment building and its neighbor.

"It's not much," she said, filling the silence, "but it's home."

He walked the two steps to the window and peered down into the alley.

Taylor grabbed a duffel bag—her only remaining piece of luggage—and went to her dresser. "We need to talk about money."

"Right," he said, turning from the window. "My offer from this morning stands. Four times what you make, plus paying off your credit card bills. And of course I'll cover any expenses."

She might be bailing him out of a tough position, but his offer was much too generous. "I'll come for expenses and a stipend, but I can't accept the money to pay off my debts. They're my debts, Jake, and I have to take care of them myself. I don't need to be rescued, just compensated for my time. And it's not as if I'm going to be working that hard. A couple of dinners with Mr. Hankins and his grandchildren is not a big deal."

"It's a big deal to me."

"I don't want charity."

"Fine. I won't pay your debts."

"Good. But there is one other thing we need to agree on. I'm definitely going to lose my job. Sleazy Steve won't forgive me for skipping off for a week without notice."

"Sleazy Steve?" Jake asked, sounding mad.

Taylor had gotten so used to her boss's nickname that she didn't even think about it anymore. But she realized it might be a little off-putting. "He has a…reputation. But don't worry, he never tried anything on me. And if he had, he would've ended up with a broken wrist. I took a self-defense class when I was living at the YWCA."

"You shouldn't be working for someone like that."

"I couldn't risk looking for another job. Any interruption in my income would have meant losing this apartment. As for finding a new job, if I can't find one right away I'm going to have to ask you to pay my rent for a month."

"That's fair," Jake said.

"And I'll need some clothes. I sold a lot of my things to get back on my feet. My wardrobe doesn't extend to entertaining dinner guests."

"We'll go shopping this evening."

"Okay. Give me a minute to pack up." She went into the bathroom for a few things, then stuffed some other necessities into the duffel bag. "All set."

"Not quite." Jake reached into the pocket of his shearling coat. He pulled out a small black velvet box.

Her rings. How could she have forgotten about her rings?

A flurry of emotions ran through her, confused her. Regret, excitement, everything in between.

Then Jake flipped back the lid. Her diamond caught the light and flashed. An odd, uncomfortable feeling settled in her stomach.

"An important part of the costume," Jake said, his tone almost light.

Her tongue seemed frozen. "Yeah," she managed.

Jake took the engagement ring and matching wedding band out of their cushion. He held them in his palm.

She held out her own hand, palm up. Jake deposited the rings into her hand.

Without touching her.

Yes, her marriage was definitely over, Taylor thought. Well and truly dead. But that would make the next week easier. Oh, there might still be a physical spark between them, some strange force drawing them together, but on an emotional level there was nothing. Big old nothing.

Slowly she closed her fingers around the rings, pretending to herself that hiding them would make this easier. She certainly didn't have the strength to put them on again, not yet.

Jake watched her for a long, excruciating moment before picking up her bag. "Let's go get you some clothes."

Taylor stared through the windshield of Jake's truck as they rounded the last bend in the drive and the ranch buildings came into view.

She couldn't believe she was back.

But here she was, back in Montana. Back at the scene of the most turbulent point in her twenty-two years.

The place looked so different, she thought. The tall

grass and wildflowers were gone, obscured by a blanket of snow, and smoke curled from every chimney in the compound. The snow made the rugged Montana landscape seem even more vast, more isolated.

Jake's parting words from the summer before echoed in her head.

You don't belong here.

Until yesterday those had been their last words for five months. Every time she'd thought of Montana in the interim, those harsh words had been right there with her.

Looking at the immense emptiness around her, it was easy to imagine he'd been right. Maybe she belonged in the city, despite the unpleasantness of her life there now.

But it didn't matter if she belonged *here* or not, she reminded herself. Her contract with Jake was for a week. One single, solitary week. Seven days. She'd do her job and then she'd get back on the plane to Boston.

Jake pulled up in front of the ranch house. She stepped carefully down onto the icy driveway and moved to the bed of the truck, unfastening the tarp to retrieve her suitcase. Last summer she would have stood by while Jake carried her suitcase, but now she wanted to stand on her own two feet.

Jake had a different idea, though. He reached to take the suitcase from her, ignoring her protest. As he did so their hands brushed accidentally and Taylor froze.

Their long day together had done nothing to lessen

the awareness between them. By tacit agreement they'd avoided physical contact ever since he'd grabbed her wrist at lunch, and by and large they'd succeeded—except for the time she'd fallen asleep on the plane and woken with her head pillowed on his shoulder.

It was too easy, too seductive, to fall back into the patterns of the summer before, when they'd been so openly and joyfully physical with each other.

But she had to keep her distance—despite the signals her body sent her.

She hung back as they walked to the porch, thinking of the first time she'd come to the ranch, as Jake's bride. Despite the beautiful scenery, at its peak in the middle of the summer, she'd had eyes only for Jake. She'd studied him as he drove, then sat and watched him as he parked the truck and walked around to her door.

He'd opened the passenger door and kissed her thoroughly before picking her up in his arms and carrying her not just over the threshold, but all the way to his bed. And then he'd carried her somewhere else entirely. Neither of them had given a thought to their luggage until several hours after dark.

Ahead of her on the porch, Jake pushed open the door. It swung inward, revealing the same neat front hall she'd stormed out of five months before.

Her footsteps halted of their own accord. Jake stood by the open door. He watched her without moving. The six feet of porch between them felt like an impassable distance.

She longed for the days when everything had been easy, when she could simply go into his arms and everything would be okay. Those days were gone. So far gone she wouldn't even get a simple "welcome home" before she stepped into the house they'd shared.

She looked into Jake's eyes, unable to read his expression. It seemed distant, almost disconnected. Then he surprised her by saying, his voice soft, "It didn't turn out like either of us expected, did it?"

Regret? It wasn't an emotion she'd expected from him, and as soon as she recognized it, it was gone. Completely gone. His face was a mask again.

But she hadn't imagined it. "No, it didn't," she said.

She stepped toward the doorway, keeping as far away from Jake as possible. It was easier that way.

As she crossed the threshold the warm scents of baking assailed her. Her mouth watered instantly. It had been so long since she'd smelled that rich, buttery smell...

Jake shut the door firmly behind them. "Irma must have made those fancy cookies you like so much." His voice was cool.

"They're called madeleines," she said, shrugging out of her new down parka, "and they're tea cakes, not cookies."

Taylor glanced around as she hung her parka on the coat tree. Through an archway she could see the living room, with its polished wood floor and solid leather furniture, arranged exactly as she remembered.

The fire crackling in the big stone hearth made it seem particularly cozy and inviting.

On the other side of the entrance hall lay the dining room. She peeked around the corner at it. A sturdy iron candelabra still sat in the center of the massive wooden table, matching the sconces that lined the walls.

The inside of the house seemed very much the same. Familiar, almost. Taylor felt a fleeting, inexplicable sense of homecoming.

She quickly dismissed it. She didn't even like it here. Her feelings about the place were *not* positive. Her dreams had been dashed here. Her life had come apart. Obviously it was only the comparison to her apartment that made it seem so wonderful.

Irma appeared in the hallway, wiping her hands on her apron. "Taylor!" She hurried over for a hug and a kiss, then stepped back to survey her. "You're skin and bones, girl. I'll have to fatten you up."

"You do that," Jake said. "I'll take Taylor's suitcase upstairs." He seemed as eager to get away from her as she was from him.

Taylor followed the middle-aged housekeeper back to the kitchen.

"I know why you're here," Irma said, sitting her down at the small round table in the corner. "Jake explained it to Orville and me." Irma's husband Orville cooked for the ranch hands. "We don't like it, but maybe you two can find a way to settle your differences. This place ain't the same without you."

Taylor laughed as lightly as she could. She didn't

want to disappoint the other woman by saying that a reconciliation was impossible. "Right. This place is *cleaner* without me, anyway."

"So what? It's emptier, too, and that's what counts." Irma set a glass of milk and a plate of shell-shaped madeleines before her, then took a seat.

Taylor savored a madeleine in unspeakable bliss. They'd been her favorite treat ever since she'd been a little girl.

"Jake's been an ornery son of a buck," Irma confided. "The man hasn't smiled more than twice since you left. He's always grouchy and complaining. No fun to be around. I almost quit three times last fall."

Jake had been upset? Why? she wondered. Because she'd wounded his pride when she'd left him, or because he'd made such a mistake in marrying her?

The two women talked for a few minutes before Jake appeared in the doorway. Taylor wiped the feather-light madeleine crumbs from her lips and stood.

"I guess I should unpack," she said.

Jake led her upstairs to the largest guest room, which sat at the opposite end of the house from the master suite. It was nicely decorated, with antique furniture and a handmade quilt on the queen-size bed, but its pleasant temperature meant more to her than its appearance.

Living in a cold apartment had been one of the hardest lessons Taylor had faced in the past five months. Until then she'd always taken her physical comfort for granted. But since November, turning up the heat would have meant not being able to pay the electric bill.

Jake crossed to her suitcase, which sat on a folding luggage rack. He popped open the latches. "Let's get your stuff put away." He transferred a couple of the new shirts he'd bought her yesterday to one of the dressers. "See if you can't keep the room clean while you're here, okay? Drawers closed, bed made. If Hankins happens to wander upstairs, I don't want him to guess you're staying in here. It wouldn't look good."

She pulled out a few items and stored them in a drawer. "I thought he was just coming to dinner a couple of times."

"That's all we've got planned. But the Hankins's place hasn't been a working ranch in a long time, and his cabin's pretty rustic. I expect he and those kids will come visit a lot."

"Oh."

"Plus, it can get boring here in wintertime." Jake shot her a pointed look. "Even more boring than in the summer. Neighborly visits help lessen that."

After the way Jake had ignored her last summer, working all day in order to avoid her, he shouldn't be talking about the benefits of neighborly visits, she thought.

He reached into her suitcase to lift out a dress. The action revealed her neatly folded camisoles and tap pants.

Their eyes met.

Even though she'd sold most of her other clothes,

she'd kept the lingerie as one of her few remaining luxuries.

Jake obviously remembered the items.

He'd used to talk about the satiny smoothness of them, the way they kept the warmth of her body, how they smelled of her skin.

Heat swamped her.

Jake picked up her favorite pale pink camisole in his work-roughened hands. She remembered how those hands had felt, caressing her through the silk. Hot. Strong. Demanding yet infinitely gentle as he peeled the flimsy top off her body.

He raised an eyebrow. "It'll be more convincing if I take a few of these and toss them around my room," he said in that whiskey-soft voice. "One on the floor, another draped over the edge of my bed..."

My bed. Her brain stuck on the words.

Taylor wondered why the phrase mattered, why it bothered her. She didn't want it to be *their* bed anymore, didn't want their marriage to be real again.

She finally knew better than to try to get love from someone who couldn't give it. Someone who, like her father and his precious business deals, or her mother and her endless quest for beauty and social status, couldn't pay attention long enough to find out who their daughter really was. Someone who was married to his damned ranch, and had only cared for his wife when it was convenient.

Or when he wanted physical gratification.

Though earthshaking, sex with Jake had always been a poor substitute for the deeper sharing and affection she'd craved, a fact he would never understand.

No, she definitely didn't want Jake back. She only wanted to complete their business deal. To make a fair wage for her week's work, and to prove she wasn't a selfish brat anymore.

Maybe she'd acted badly last summer, but she'd changed. She'd realized her mistakes, one of which had been going after Jake in the first place. Now she was ready to release the past, redeem herself and move on.

Taylor reached for the camisole. "I don't think so, Jake." As he watched, she painstakingly refolded it the way she'd learned during her brief stint in a clothing store last fall, before she'd been fired and had looked for work as a waitress. She laid it in a drawer. "You just keep your door closed down the hall. I'll make sure this room looks vacant. We'll be fine."

She quickly unpacked the rest of her things, then tucked the suitcase and luggage rack in the back of the closet. All her belongings had fit into one of the two dressers. The room looked untouched.

"Just like a hotel room," she muttered.

"Keep it that way."

"Yes, sir," she said, saluting his broad back as he strode from the room.

An hour later she joined him for a sumptuous dinner cooked by Irma. They sat at opposite ends of the long table, not close together as they had last summer.

The iron candelabra partially obscured their views of each other, preventing any feeling of intimacy.

Which was fine with her. She wanted to eat, not stare adoringly into her husband's eyes.

They dined in silence until halfway through dessert, when someone pounded on the front door.

As Irma went to answer it Jake murmured, "Must be Hankins, stopping by to say hello. Ready to face the music?"

Taylor glanced down at the diamond wedding set on her left hand. The gems sparkled in the flickering candlelight. Simple and elegant, they looked just right. As if they belonged on her hand.

It had been hard to put them back on. Hard to wear them again considering everything they represented. Hope. Failure.

She remembered Jake's proposal, when he'd slipped the engagement ring on her finger at midnight on the stern deck of a cruise ship. Remembered their wedding, and the confident touch of his fingers as he put his wedding band on her. Remembered ripping the rings off her finger and throwing them at him right before she stormed off the ranch.

Taylor gulped. With the deception upon them, she felt a moment's unease. But it was too late to back out.

"Sure," she said. "I'm ready."

Sounds carried from the front hall: the door opening and closing, footsteps and voices.

She heard Irma's surprised exclamations, a man's hearty laugh and a child saying, "I'm hungry! Is this where we get to eat?"

Jake stood. "Shall we see what's going on?"

He circled the table and helped her from her chair. He steered her from the dining room, his hand resting possessively at the small of her back.

Taylor felt herself slip into the deception. She pretended she loved her husband, allowed her back to melt against the warmth of his hand. She imagined she couldn't wait to be alone with him later that night.

Then they turned the corner.

Chaos reigned in the front hall. Piles of luggage surrounded Irma and four newcomers. Taylor's startled gaze went from Henry Hankins to a red-haired girl to two boys, one of whom balanced a leather flight bag on his head while the other swung a yo-yo in wild circles, barely missing the overhead light fixture.

Hankins spread his arms wide. "Hey there, Cassidy!" He stepped forward to shake hands. "And hello to you, too, little lady. Y'all sure are a sight for sore eyes." He winked at Taylor. "Especially you, darlin'. Your husband ain't quite so perty."

She smiled at the sprightly old Texan. "Nice to see you again, Mr. Hankins."

"Oh, call me Hank," he boomed. "We're practically family now, so no more of that formal stuff." He handed Irma his hat and coat. "Sorry to drop in on you like this, Cassidy, but we've got a little problem. Furnace conked out. My place is an icebox and the woodstove hain't worked in decades. Guess we'll have to stay here a few days." He picked up two large suitcases. "Point us to your guest rooms, partner."

Chapter Three

Without waiting for an answer, Henry "Hank" Hankins headed for the stairs with his luggage.

Caught off guard, Jake took a moment to react.

Guess we'll have to stay here. Hank and his grandchildren were going to be their houseguests.

Oh, God.

He glanced over at his wife, who stared back at him with wide eyes. He could tell they were both thinking the same thing: her clothes were in one of the guest bedrooms. And that thought led straight to another more dangerous thought.

He and Taylor were going to have to share his bedroom.

After what Hank had seen last summer—a couple who were madly in love and couldn't keep their hands off each other—he would never believe she'd moved out of the master suite. They had no choice, not if Jake wanted to buy that range land.

But would Taylor go along with it? One word from her and his whole deception would blow up.

He shot her an entreating look, silently begging her to go along with him for now and work out the details later.

She nodded almost imperceptibly. Thank goodness. Jake put his mind to the problem at hand: stopping Hank before he got to the spare bedrooms. Before he found the one that held Taylor's insanely sexy underclothes, as well as the rest of her belongings.

"Hank," he said, "hold on a minute."

The older man stopped with his foot on the bottom stair. He set down his cases and slapped his head. "Holy hail, where are my manners? I forgot to introduce y'all!" Marching back over to them, he said, "This perty gal's my granddaughter, Melissa. She lives in See-attle with all them punk rockers."

Melissa, who looked about fourteen, gave them a wry, embarrassed smile.

"I got her to come look after these Texas rug rats. That's Frankie and the other one's Billy. They're brothers. Frankie, get your finger outta your nose and shake the man's hand!"

Jake greeted the boys, making a mental note to wash his hands as soon as possible. He looked over at Taylor, who seemed to be holding back a grin.

"All right. Did that." Hank picked up his bags.

Jake gave a silent groan. So much for Plan A. Time

to put Plan B into action. Except there was no Plan B.

Taylor stepped in to save the day. "Mr. Hankins…" she said in her softest debutante's voice.

Hank beamed at her, instantly enthralled. Just as he'd been last summer, when he'd hung on her every word. "Hank, little lady. Jest Hank."

"All right, Hank. You see, there's a small problem… The guest rooms aren't exactly ready." She said it with the chagrin of a woman who prided herself on her housekeeping.

Jake sent her a grateful look. The woman was a better actress than she thought.

Hank waved away Taylor's concerns. "Don't you worry about the guest rooms. We can make our own beds if it comes to that."

So much for Plan B.

Jake positioned himself in front of the stairs, blocking their path. "How about you all have a little supper first," he suggested as casually as he could. "Irma, have you got anything to feed our guests?"

The housekeeper clucked her tongue at him. "Of course I do!" She looked at Hank. "What would you like? A steak?"

"Sounds great," Hank said. "But not right now. Melissa and I had best get these things out of the front hall. The boys are probably hungry, though."

Nice try, Jake thought.

Irma, unfazed, turned to the boys. "Hamburgers for the two of you?"

Frankie shrugged his agreement, but Billy said, "I hate hamburgers."

Hank looked embarrassed. "Red meat makes the boy throw up. No explanation for it, but it's a guaranteed event."

"Chicken soup?" suggested Irma.

Frankie made a face. "I want mac and cheese."

Irma nodded. "Suits me. Now, you boys come on back to the kitchen and tell me about your trip while you wash your hands."

Irma departed, the two boys in tow. Which left them with the same problem they'd had a minute ago.

Once again, Taylor stepped into the breach. "There's a fire in the living room," she said, moving toward the stairs. "Why don't you warm yourselves up while I get everything ready?"

"Not on a bet, little lady," Hank said. "I've made my bed before, and I can do it again. I don't intend for us to be any trouble."

Jake wanted to pick the man up and deposit him on one of the big leather chairs by the hearth. And maybe strap him to it. "It's no problem for Taylor to get the guest rooms ready, Hank. Come have a seat. You too, Melissa." It was more an order than a request.

Hank moved toward the stairs. "First I'll put my bags away."

"Grandpa," Melissa began, trying to stop him.

"Bring your stuff, sweatpea. We'll grab the boys' things in a couple minutes."

Taylor glanced helplessly over at him.

He shrugged, giving in to the unavoidable. "Fine," he said. "We'll get you settled." If they played their cards right, they might still be able to keep Hank from noticing anything amiss.

Might be able to.

Jake refused to consider the alternative.

Upstairs, he tried to steer Hank away from Taylor's room, thinking that if Melissa took the room instead, it would be easier to get Taylor's things out.

But he wasn't successful. "Never did care about having a view of the sunrise," Hank said, dismissing the room Jake suggested. "You give that one to Melissa. I'll take this one here." Short of tackling and hog-tying him, Jake couldn't deter him from his chosen course.

Behind Hank's back, Taylor rolled her eyes to the ceiling and took Melissa off down the hall.

Jake stayed with Hank. Pretending to be an obliging, overprotective host, he reached into the closet for the luggage rack. Surreptitiously, he nudged Taylor's empty suitcase another few inches out of sight.

He unfolded the luggage rack, saying, "Set one of those bags on this and then we'll go sit by the fire."

Ignoring his suggestion, Hank unzipped the first suitcase.

Disaster. The man planned to unpack.

Taylor reappeared, realized what was going on and gave Jake a horrified look. He held her gaze, sending her a silent message.

It got through loud and clear.

Quickly she stationed herself in front of the dresser

they'd filled just that afternoon, blocking Hank's access. She leaned negligently against it, her face a mask of unconcern. With luck, Hank would automatically use the other dresser.

Jake grinned at her. They were working well together.

Taylor jerked her head toward the connecting bathroom. She made a little motion, as if pulling out a drawer.

Her toiletries. She must have stowed them in the bathroom already.

Jake cleared his throat. "I think I'll, uh, wash my hands."

Hank looked up from his suitcase. "Good idea, son."

Jake slipped into the bathroom, closing the door behind him. Just as Taylor had promised, a cursory inspection yielded no signs of habitation. But the second drawer of the vanity held her newly purchased toiletry kit.

He stepped back into the bedroom, holding the kit behind his back.

Jake didn't think he could make it if he tried to dash across the room. He waited for just the right moment, when Hank had his head in the closet, and lobbed the bag to Taylor.

She caught it silently and jammed it behind her back.

Hank continued unpacking, distributing his clothes between the closet and the empty dresser. Taylor asked him what he'd been up to since the summer.

Hank told her all about some oil deal he'd put together in South America.

The dresser filled rapidly. Most of the way through
the second suitcase, it reached capacity. Jake saw
Hank's gaze shift to the dresser Taylor protected with
her body.

But the next item out of the bag was a leather toiletry case.

Hank headed for the bathroom.

Jake jerked his chin at Taylor, but she didn't need
the signal. She whipped open the drawer with most
of her intimate items in it, scooped the whole lot up
in her arms, balanced her own toiletry kit on top, and
slipped into the hall on her quick little feet.

Not a moment too soon.

Hank returned. "Where'd your gal go?" he asked.
"I wasn't finished telling her about Bolivia."

Jake told him he thought she'd gone to see to the
boys' bedroom.

She'd left the drawer open. Hank put the rest of his
clothes into it. Jake held his breath until the last item
fit neatly inside.

Hank lined up his shoes on the closet floor, closed
his suitcases and dusted off his hands. "See?" he
said. "That wasn't so bad."

Taylor and Melissa appeared in the doorway. Taylor shot him a questioning look. Had they made it?

Yes, they'd made it.

Tension flowed out of her body. She grinned at
him, happy with the success of their deception. Her
smile hit him in the gut, hard. For a few minutes

they'd been playing on the same team, working together to solve a problem. It felt so effortless, so natural. So much like last summer, before things had fallen apart.

Hank turned to Taylor. "Can't figure what you were so worried about. This room's perty as a picture. Y'all should run one of them bread-and-breakfast places," he said. "Since your guest rooms are so nice."

"That's *bed*-and-breakfast, Grandpa."

"Whatever." Hank slapped Jake on the back, making him stumble a few steps forward. "Let's go sit by that fire, son."

When they headed downstairs, Taylor lingered in the upstairs hallway. From the corner of his eye Jake saw her dart back into Hank's room.

Good. She could clear out the rest of her stuff. They'd be safe, at least temporarily.

But could they keep up the pretense of being lovingly married once they had to share the master suite? Once her clothes sat next to his in the dresser and her towel hung next to his on the rack? Once they took their showers in the same bathtub, the tub where, last summer, they'd—

Jake drew himself up short. He wanted to lose his head with her, take her in his arms the way he'd used to, hold her and kiss her and feel her body responding to his touch. But drifting off into memories of making love to his wife wasn't going to help him survive this week. He had to put the past behind him.

* * *

Four hours later, Taylor collapsed onto one of the chairs in Jake's bedroom. She sprawled out her legs and let her arms droop over the sides of the armrests. Exhaustion washed over her—major exhaustion, as if she'd worked a double shift at the restaurant—and her eyes closed of their own accord.

To her left the other chair creaked as Jake settled his weight onto it. He made a noise—half groan, half sigh.

She didn't bother to open her eyes. "You owe me, Jake. Big time."

"I know."

Who'd have thought hosting a few houseguests could be so taxing? She'd never really *had* houseguests before. Not of her own, anyway. She'd barely graduated from college when she'd met Jake. As a student she'd lived in the sorority house. The only time she'd ever had her own apartment was the last few months. But her apartment wasn't the kind of place where you entertained.

Of course, it was probably easier to deal with houseguests when you weren't trying to pull a hoax on them. That had been the exhausting part.

At the same time, though, their charade tonight had formed a bond between herself and Jake. They were conspirators now, not just separated spouses. It made it easier to relate to him.

"Did Hank call to have his furnace fixed?" she asked, eyes still closed.

"There's no rush," Jake said. "They aren't going back to the cabin this week. Couldn't you tell?"

She could. Even Hank wouldn't have unpacked quite so much for just one night. But she hadn't wanted to face what it meant.

It was one thing to play the adoring wife for a few dinners, but to have to do it twenty-four hours a day... If she'd known—or even imagined—that something like this might happen, she never would have left her crummy apartment.

"This is great," she said. "We're on marriage duty all week long. We'll have to share this bedroom—" She stopped.

"All week long. I know." There was silence, then, "I'm sorry for the change of plans, Taylor."

The apology startled her. He sounded serious, she thought. Genuinely sorry.

She rolled her head to stare at him. He lay back just as she did, his long legs stretched out in front of him, his arms hanging toward the floor. Eyes closed, he looked utterly spent.

And utterly sexy. As if he'd just spent the night making love to her.

Suddenly Taylor shivered. She shouldn't be thinking such thoughts. She couldn't afford to lose her head. This week was her chance to redeem herself, to prove she'd changed, and she couldn't do that if she let herself get sidetracked.

She forced her mind back to their conversation. "Apology accepted," she said, her gaze fixed firmly on the ceiling.

Jake cleared his throat. "I think we need to renegotiate our terms."

"Oh?" Surprise made her answer quickly.

"Yeah. Your job description just got a lot more complicated. I think your salary needs to reflect that."

"Uh, Jake…"

"Hank said he'd take a few thousand off the price of the land to make up for the inconvenience of their visit and the busted furnace. The money should be yours."

"I want to take care of my debts on my own." And unfortunately, even a few thousand dollars wouldn't take care of all her debts.

"As hard as you'll be working this week, you'll earn that money fair and square. I won't take no for an answer."

It wasn't worth fighting about. "Fine. You'll get your money's worth."

They sat in silence for a long moment, exhausted by the effort of speech.

Finally he opened one eye and stared at her. "I almost hate to mention this, but Hank's going to expect to see some displays of affection. Some hugs and kisses."

She groaned. "Tell me you're not linking that to the extra money."

"I'm not," he said, his voice suddenly rough and smoky. "Unless you'd like me to…"

Her pulse jumped. "Look," she said, "even if you could afford—"

He laughed. It was deep and warm. She hadn't heard him laugh that way since the summer, since they'd been in love.

She needed distance. "Okay," she said, standing up. "Hugs and kisses. In public."

"And a few caresses. If necessary."

Caresses. She could almost feel his hand stroking her skin. "If absolutely necessary," she said. At the bed, she looked down at her piles of clothes. She seized the excuse to change the subject. "Where do you want my things?"

He'd turned to watch her, no longer looking so exhausted.

"And before you get in a snit about how messy I am," she continued, "remember that I brought this stuff in here in a hurry and haven't had a moment to clean it up since."

"I wasn't going to say that."

But she knew he was thinking it. She'd seen how his eyes had fixed on the bed when they'd first come upstairs, before she'd collapsed into her chair. "Where do you want them?"

"How about where you had them last summer?"

Taylor glanced over at the dresser she'd used. It stood in exactly the same place against the wall. The drawers she'd overturned above her suitcase last summer were back in their slots.

She glanced around, really seeing the room for the first time. Everything else looked the same, too. Nothing had changed in five months. Even her Bristol bowl of potpourri still sat on the mantel between the two brass candlesticks one of her distant relatives had given them as wedding presents.

And on the nightstand, still, was the picture of them

that Jake's aunt K.D., who lived in Wyoming, had taken on the cruise ship two days before they got married. In each other's arms, giddy with new love.

Taylor wondered briefly why he hadn't removed the picture but then reminded herself that Jake didn't care much about his immediate environment, as long as it was neat and clean. He probably hadn't even looked at it since she'd left.

Her survey of the room finished, Taylor picked up a small stack of clothes and crossed to the dresser. She refolded the items and tucked them into the empty drawers.

Two trips later, Jake murmured, "You don't have to go overboard."

"Is it a crime to fold my clothes?"

"I don't care how messy your clothes are as long as they're in the drawers, not spread out on the floor."

She pointed toward the heavy wood door to his room. "Once that door closes, I'm off the clock. Anything I do in here is for me, not you."

She went to the bed for the final stack of clothes, turning her back on him to fold them.

She heard his chair creak as he levered himself out of it. He walked across the room and into the bathroom, closing the door behind him.

Taylor kept folding.

The shower came on, its noise muted by the bathroom door.

It brought back memories. Memories of warm summer nights of lovemaking. Memories of the effortless intimacy they'd shared in this room.

But only while making love. Aside from that they'd never developed the kind of intimacy that made a marriage last, the knowledge of each other that would carry them through the hard times when physical desire alone couldn't do it anymore.

She closed the last drawer, then padded over to the mantel and leaned down to sniff the bowl of potpourri. Nothing. The scents of lavender and rose had long since faded.

Which probably explained why Jake hadn't gotten rid of it, she thought wryly. Last summer he'd done nothing but complain about the smell.

Going to the window at the front of the house, she pushed aside the curtains and peered out over the snowy landscape. Lights shone onto the snow from some of the ranch hands' cabins. A slice of moon illuminated the sweep of country around the ranch, but left the sky dark enough that she could see stars.

She took a deep breath. This was so unlike the view from her tiny apartment in Boston—of that back alley filled with trash and broken bottles. And the stars didn't seem to shine on her neighborhood.

Compared to her exciting life in Boston before she'd married Jake, the country had seemed empty and desolate. But it had its attractions compared to a dingy slum. Space, freedom, clean air.

She didn't hear the shower go off or the bathroom door open.

"It's only for a week, Taylor."

She turned, releasing the curtains. Had she been looking that despondent?

Jake stood in the bathroom doorway, a towel wrapped around his hips and his clothes in his hands. His dark hair was tousled. She knew he'd just run the towel roughly over it to dry it.

She swallowed, forgetting all about Boston. He was so appealing, so sexy.

So close.

"It'll go faster than you think."

She was sure it would. But would it go faster than she wanted it to? she wondered. That was the danger, especially with Jake mostly naked and only a few feet away.

It would be so easy just to walk toward him and into his embrace. To feel his strong arms wrap around her. To be safe, at least temporarily.

So many times this fall she'd lain in her cold bed wishing things could have worked out. If Jake had been able to give her more than the comfort of his body, they might have had a chance.

Looking at him now, she almost thought she'd be willing to take the bargain she hadn't been able to accept last summer. She would have his body and a warm, wonderful house. She would live in a beautiful, rugged landscape, with clean air and nature all around. She wouldn't have to carry pepper spray in her pocket, or worry about dying in a drive-by shooting.

The price? A husband who didn't truly love her. Who overlooked her. Who avoided emotional intimacy. A husband who worked hard on his ranch but left her to wander around the house all day with nothing to do and nowhere to go.

Yes, it almost looked like a fair bargain. But she didn't take it. Deliberately, knowing she was making the right choice, she walked around the bed, picked up her toiletry kit, and slipped past Jake into the bathroom.

Steam covered the bathroom mirrors. The air was hot and damp. It smelled of the woodsy soap Jake used. She felt the scent settling around her, enveloping her.

Temptation returned. She loved the smell of his body, the feel of his skin. She'd never been able to get enough of touching him.

She washed her face and brushed her teeth, then realized she hadn't brought her nightclothes with her to the bathroom.

Old habits died hard.

Her body obviously thought nothing had changed, that they were going through their usual bedtime routine and would soon be in bed together, making love.

It was all the push she needed to make a firm decision. She might be tempted, but she was not going to sleep with her husband.

She'd gotten into this mess of a marriage by letting herself get caught up in her physical desires, by not thinking. Repeating the past wouldn't make things better.

Still clothed, she darted out of the bathroom to get her nightshirt. Jake, she noticed, now wore only boxers.

How could she not notice? Jake's bare torso seemed to take up half the space in the sizable room. And something had happened to all the air, too.

She grabbed a shirt and a pair of silk boxers and headed back to the relative safety of the bathroom.

No sooner had she slipped the T-shirt over her head than she realized her mistake. The shirt was one of his, soft and faded, with the words Cassidy's Dry Goods stenciled across the front. It was from his aunt K.D.'s store down South. The fabric was so broken in that it was almost nonexistent. Despite the shirt's large size, it concealed little.

Taking a deep breath for courage, she opened the bathroom door.

Jake stood on the far side of the bed, a blanket in his hands. He glanced over at her before going back to making his bed. He laid the blanket on the rug, spread a sheet over it, then folded both in two and tucked two edges under to make a sleeping sack.

Taylor took her dirty clothes to the closet and put them in the hamper—something she'd never done while she lived here before, she realized.

Jake pulled a pillow from the bed and tossed it to the end of his bedroll. "I wondered where that shirt had gotten to."

"Sorry," she said.

"No big deal." He met her eyes, then his gaze roved lazily over her body. "It always looked better on you anyway."

She swallowed, hard, fighting the urge to cross her arms over her chest. "Who gets the bed?"

"You do." He motioned toward his bedroll. "Though looking at this, I'm tempted to ask you to share."

"Not a good idea, Jake."

"I know. The bed's all yours."

"Thank you."

"Consider it part of your payment."

She climbed in. The sheets smelled of Jake, and the effect was even more overpowering than the steamy air of the bathroom had been.

She was in his bed. The one place on his entire ranch where she'd felt safe and protected and loved. The sheets caressed the contours of her body. The blankets and comforter settled over her, their weight adding to the feeling of comfort.

Not enough weight, though. Not nearly enough.

How was she ever going to be able to sleep?

She turned out the light, but couldn't help watching in the dimness as Jake folded his long body into his makeshift bed. There wasn't much cushioning between him and the floor.

"Don't you have a pad to sleep on?" she asked.

"My gear is in the basement. I thought it might look odd if I brought it all up here tonight."

Good point. "That just doesn't look very comfortable."

"It's not. But unless you want to share the bed, Taylor…"

She should have just kept her mouth shut. "No. No, that's okay," she said quickly. "I guess it's the same as when you're on a cattle drive, right?"

"Right. Exactly the same."

She pulled the sheets to her chin and stared at the ceiling. "Will you be warm enough?"

"Is that an offer, Taylor?"

A hot flush overtook her entire body. If he joined her in the middle of the night, when she was sleeping, then it would be his weakness that got them back into trouble, not hers. But as appealing as it might be, that path led only to disaster and unpleasantness. "Of an extra blanket. Nothing more."

"Uh-huh."

"Climb into this bed and die, Jake."

Chapter Four

Jake left Taylor fast asleep in his bed early the next morning.

Seeing her there brought it all back. Her hair spread out on the pillow, the sheets tracing the shape of her body, her deep, even, quiet breathing.

God, but it was hard to have her back. Thank goodness he could throw himself into his work the way he had last summer. It was the only way to maintain his balance, the only way to keep her from overwhelming him.

He went downstairs, through the quiet house, and out into the cold darkness. Clouds had moved in overnight, blocking his view of the stars. These were the shortest days of the year, and they couldn't wait for dawn before starting work.

In the cookhouse, Jake grabbed a cup of Orville's black-as-mud coffee and a plate of bacon and eggs.

He sat with his hands at the long dining table. They ate and talked and watched the weather forecast on the old television set in the corner.

Jake glanced around the table at his ranch hands, who were some of the finest workers around. Put together they could handle any job the operation needed, from fixing a cranky diesel engine to telling at a glance which cows in a herd were in heat. Two of them, including his best mechanic, were women.

He hung on to them by paying them well and treating them right. He couldn't imagine letting any of them go, but that was what he'd have to do if Hank didn't sell him the land.

Which ones, though? Reid had been here the shortest time, but he had a magic touch with horses. Without Dusty he'd never keep the fleet of vehicles running. If Ty left, taking his doctoring skills with him, Jake didn't doubt they'd lose a few extra animals during calving season. The problem was the same for all his other hands.

He wouldn't have to lay off anyone if he got the land, though. So all he had to do was make sure Hank believed he and Taylor were happily married and madly in love. By whatever means it took.

For an hour or so after breakfast Jake and Reid worked with the horses in the brightly lit barn. Together they mucked out stalls and distributed hay and grain. One of the mares had a slow-healing cut near one of her front hooves, so Jake soaked the wound in a bucket of antiseptic solution and changed the bandage.

By the time he'd finished holding the willful mare's leg in the bucket, the sun was up, though hidden behind the heavy clouds. He left Reid in the barn and took one of his new cutting horses out to stretch his legs.

When he returned to the barn, he found Taylor in the tack room, riding herd on Frankie and Billy. Her presence there surprised him. He hadn't really expected her to leave the house all week.

Jake pushed back the sleeve of his heavy stockman's coat to check his wristwatch. Seven-fifty. Early, for Taylor, even with the time difference to Boston. Especially to be clean and dressed, considering she spent almost twenty minutes in the shower each day.

He stood quietly in the doorway as she told her not-so-attentive audience all about the tack and equipment hanging on the walls.

Frankie caught sight of Jake first. "Hey, Mr. Cassidy!"

Taylor whipped around. "Oh, hi, Jake."

Surprise brought a sudden hint of pink to her cheeks. She looked adorable. Irresistible.

Unable to stop himself, he crossed to her in two easy strides. "Good morning, Taylor." Bending his head, he gave her a quick kiss on her soft, warm lips.

Just a little innocent affection between husband and wife, but it felt surprisingly good.

Too good. He wanted to give her more than just a good-morning peck, but he didn't think their young audience would appreciate it.

Taylor pulled back, her flush deepening. "Excuse me?"

"Practice," he murmured low enough so the boys wouldn't hear.

She frowned at him.

"I know, it's the last thing we need. But we had to start sometime." He turned to the boys. "How long have you been up?"

"Hours and hours," answered Billy. He pulled his yo-yo from his pocket and whirled it around his head.

"They were getting restless," Taylor explained, ducking. "And Melissa needed a break."

Out of the corner of his eye, Jake saw Frankie pick up a screwdriver from a shelf and begin to pry on the hinges of the cabinet where they kept the medical supplies for the horses. He shepherded both boys out of the tack room. "Why don't we show them the goats?"

"Goats?" Taylor asked, obviously not knowing what he was talking about. She covered her mistake. "Oh, the goats. For a second I thought you meant the, uh, mountain goats."

They walked the length of the barn, skirting the huge stack of hay bales to reach the stall where two goats now lived. Jake tossed them some food from a bucket hanging on the door and let the boys in.

The stall smelled of goat, but Frankie and Billy didn't mind. The two animals, one black and one brown, made their goaty noises and blinked at the boys.

The boys, in turn, made excited boy noises and approached the goats.

Taylor leaned over the edge of the stall, her elbows on the weathered wood. She watched for a moment, then joined Jake where he stood leaning against the hay bales a few feet away.

"Since when?" she asked, her voice a murmur.

"November. Orville talked me into it." He nodded toward the boys. "Thanks for looking after them, Taylor."

She shrugged. "It was either bring them out here or have them tear apart the house while Melissa showered. I'm hoping they'll settle down a bit after breakfast."

"Not likely."

"Yeah, I know."

Jake watched the boys for a minute, surprised and pleased to see how gentle they were with the animals. Obviously they only liked to destroy inanimate objects.

"Are you going to come in for breakfast?"

He shook his head. "I already ate. Anyway, I'll be pretty busy today. The weather service says we might get a storm in the next few days."

"A bad one?"

"Hard to say. It could blow by to the north. But we're taking precautions."

Taylor nodded. She stepped into the stall and disentangled the boys from the goats. The word "waffles" was enough to send them running helter-skelter from the barn.

She followed, not running.

Jake checked the latch on the stall door and caught up with her. Their steps crunched in the snow as they headed for the house.

Taylor looked up at him. "I thought you weren't coming to breakfast."

"I want to make sure Irma's got everything she needs in case we get that storm."

Hank met them at the front door. "Up with the chickens, are ya?"

"Morning, Hank," Jake said. "Ready for breakfast?"

"Yup. This country air sure works up my appetite. I jest saw them two boys fly past, so I guess we'll be eatin' somethin' good."

Taylor picked the boys' jackets off the front hall floor and lined their boots up against the wall.

Jake stared. That was *Taylor* picking up someone else's clothes? Taylor? He could hardly believe his eyes.

But come to think of it, she wasn't as messy as she used to be. She'd even put away her dirty clothes the night before. And her apartment in Boston hadn't been untidy, either.

Taylor and Hank went into the dining room, where Melissa was getting the boys settled at the table.

Jake walked through to the kitchen. He checked in with Irma and wrote down the items she needed. In the basement he reviewed their emergency supplies, then went out back and made sure the generator was ready to go.

He took his time.

When he went back inside, pandemonium was in full swing. Frankie constructed a waffle fort while Billy ate with one hand and played with his yo-yo with the other, unaware of the syrup that dripped in his lap with every bite. Melissa valiantly tried to keep the boys in line, but it was a losing battle. Meanwhile Hank blithely ate his breakfast, and Taylor, looking frazzled, tried to pretend she wasn't there.

Catching sight of him, Hank said, "Jake, Taylor here tells me we might have a storm. That true?"

Jake crossed to the sideboard and poured himself a mug of coffee from the insulated carafe. "There's a good chance of it."

Hank beamed. "What luck! My grandsons hain't ever been in a real snowstorm before." He addressed the boys. "You're in for a treat. The snow's going to pile up around the house so high we won't be able to leave for days, maybe weeks!"

Melissa wilted visibly.

"It won't be that bad," Jake said, trying to reassure her. He caught Taylor's gaze. "Can I speak with you a moment?"

"Sure." She stood, giving him a bright, completely fake smile that took his breath away nonetheless.

Hank chortled. "Hoowee! Guess we know what he wants to talk about. Plans to steal some sugar, I bet."

Jake led Taylor out of the room and down the hallway to his office.

Once there, he threw himself into his office chair and picked up the phone. He got Orville on the line down at the cookhouse, told him what Irma needed, and asked him to send someone to town for supplies.

When he hung up, Taylor was standing on the far side of his desk, watching him and looking annoyed. "I thought you wanted to talk to me."

"No, that was just for Hank's benefit. So he'd think I stole you away to fool around for a few minutes. Like the old days. Since he jumped to the right conclusion, we don't actually have to do it."

"We wouldn't do it no matter what. I'm only going to kiss you in public, Jake."

"Hank's got to believe we're crazy about each other. Why don't you muss up your hair a little bit, or pinch your cheeks to get some nice color in them? Maybe undo that top button."

Taylor blew out a stream of air. "You want mussed? Okay." She undid her two top buttons, revealing a tiny slice of peach silk camisole, then tugged her shirt loose on one side. She bent over, shook out her hair and ruffled it with both hands. She must have clamped her lips together, too, because when she straightened they looked all pink and well-kissed.

She looked more than mussed. She looked like a woman who'd just had a good tumble with her husband, a husband who'd had to kiss her hard to keep her cries of fulfillment from scandalizing the whole household.

He ached.

"Taylor, I think that's taking it a bit far."

"Oh?" She did up one button. "Better?"

Worse. He couldn't see the peach silk anymore, but he knew it was there. The ache deepened. ''Taylor, you're tormenting me.''

''Good. You deserve it. How do you think I feel trying to eat a meal with those two little heathens?''

''You liked them fine in the barn.''

''I like them fine in small doses. Fifteen minutes is about all I can handle.''

He empathized, but suddenly he was enjoying their argument too much to say so. ''Ignore them. Go read a book or watch television.''

''And leave Melissa to be completely miserable?''

''You would have last summer.''

She clenched her jaw. ''That is so untrue.''

''Look, Taylor,'' he baited, ''what's your point? You want me to play baby-sitter all day long?''

She glared at him, her hands fisted on her hips. ''You want the land, Jake. To get it, you have to keep Hank happy, which means keeping me happy. That's only going to happen if you don't spend fourteen hours every day enjoying yourself in the great outdoors. So you either get your fanny inside this house at least half of every day, or you kiss that land good-bye. Got it?''

''Come here.'' He said it without thinking, the words slipping over his tongue the way her silk tops used to slip through his fingers.

''What?'' Her voice dropped half an octave, coming out all low and breathy. The way it had when they'd...

''Come here.'' He couldn't stop the words.

They stared at each other. Tension zinged through the air.

How could a situation change so quickly? One moment they'd been arguing, the next he wanted her with a need that had no limits, no boundaries. Of course, it was a familiar pattern from their marriage, one they'd both fallen victim to many times.

Jake swallowed. He'd forgotten himself. For just a moment he'd forgotten their resurrected marriage was a pretense, that he couldn't have her anymore.

Taylor took a half step forward then stopped, as if she, too, had come to her senses. She crossed her arms in front of her. "Jake," she began, then cleared her throat. Her voice came out a little more normal. More quelling. "Jake, this isn't five months ago."

Didn't he know it. "Five months ago I'd have had your shirt off by now."

Even as he said the words the image of Taylor, shirtless, popped into his mind. Jake saw her in her lacy little camisole, saw himself slip one of the spaghetti straps from her shoulder, exposing the curve of her breast. He felt the soft heat of her skin, felt her excitement.

He heard Taylor catch her breath. Again they stared at each other, silently acknowledging the flare of heat between them. It was just as strong as it had been that day on the beach, six months ago, the first time they'd met.

One touch, he thought. One touch and they wouldn't be able to stop. That was all it would take.

He was tempted. It would be so easy to turn off

his brain and let his hormones take over. Heaven knew he'd done that plenty of times last summer.

But he couldn't let himself be that weak. Not anymore. He'd learned his lesson, hadn't he?

Sure he had.

Taylor wasn't the woman for him, and never would be. She'd never be happy at the ranch. She'd never be happy living with him here, and he didn't want to spend his days wondering when she would leave again.

Jake shifted on his chair, trying to ease the tightness in his jeans. "Sorry," he muttered, annoyed with himself—and with her—for making him want her so much despite his better judgment. "I shouldn't have said that."

She nodded in agreement. "It'll only make things more difficult if we keep dredging up the past." Her voice was emphatic.

"Right," he said, feeling tired.

"Because nothing's going to happen."

"Right."

Taylor's shoulders relaxed. She leaned against the big leather armchair several feet away.

"Except in public," Jake said. But at least then they'd be safe. With other people around it couldn't get too out of hand. They couldn't do anything too stupid.

"Right. I should get back to breakfast." She straightened and headed for the door.

"Taylor."

She stopped, her hand on the knob.

"You're still a bit too mussed."

She closed her eyes briefly. Then, as he watched in fascination, she tucked in her shirt and smoothed her hair, transforming herself from a well-tossed lover into a slightly disarrayed wife in a matter of seconds. He wondered if she'd learned how to do that at her fancy women's college.

"Better?"

"Yes. I'll join you."

"Thanks." She opened the door, then added, "Do us both a favor, Jake. Don't kiss me unless it's absolutely necessary."

By the time Irma served up a wonderful dinner of roast beef, baked potatoes and vegetables that night, Taylor had begun to regret her insistence that Jake stay in the house.

She liked having him around to participate in the misery of dealing with Frankie and Billy, and to keep Hank from sharing the child-rearing expertise he'd obviously passed on to the boys' parents. But she didn't like the way he upset her equilibrium, the way he made her remember again and again the hot flush of desire she'd felt that morning.

And she didn't like the smoldering looks he kept shooting her whenever Hank was around. Rather than look at him, she kept her eyes trained on the boys as much as possible.

They'd insisted on having macaroni and cheese again, since roast beef was out of the question. As they'd grown more tired during the day, the boys had let their manners go from rudimentary at breakfast to almost nonexistent at dinner.

Her interest in them didn't escape Hank's notice. "Thinking about having some of your own?" he asked from his seat at her left.

She blinked. "Macaroni?"

"No, rug rats."

"Oh. Actually, I was wondering when Frankie was going to take that noodle out of his nose."

"Frankie!" said Melissa. To Taylor she added, for about the fiftieth time that day, "I'm so sorry."

"Stop playing with your food, son."

"Okay, Grandpa." Frankie's voice came out muted, as if he had a bad cold.

Taylor felt both fascinated and appalled. Until last night, she'd never seen anything like it. At her parents' table, the utmost decorum always prevailed. And food went directly from plate to mouth.

"So," Hank said, unfazed, "why *haven't* you started your brood yet? I figured you'd be as big as a house by now, Taylor. And I mean that in the best way." He squinted at her. "Yup, pregnancy would suit ya. Wouldn't it, Jake?"

Jake met her eyes across the length of the table, then raked his gaze briefly downward. "Yes. Yes, it would." He grinned at her like a man madly in love with his wife—like a man who couldn't wait to take his wife upstairs and get her pregnant.

Taylor sucked in her breath as she felt the impact of that grin. Awareness and arousal rocketed through her.

Jake was just playing a part, putting on a show for Hank.

But it felt so real, just as it had all day.

Hank chuckled. "Nothing like making a baby to-gether to see-ment your passion for each other. Are you blushin', gal? You don't have any good news to announce, do you?"

Taylor almost choked on a sip of wine. "I—I'm not pregnant, Hank."

Her flush deepened as Hank's gaze flicked between herself and Jake. He was obviously remembering the way they'd behaved last summer. The lust they hadn't been able to hide.

Once, when he'd been over for dinner, he'd caught them necking in the pantry. Taylor was supposed to be helping Irma with dessert, and Jake was heading to the basement for a bottle of port. But somehow they'd bumped into each other, gotten all tangled up, and had knocked a jar of olives onto the floor. Neither had noticed until both Irma and Hank had burst in on them.

No wonder Hank had thought she'd be pregnant by now.

If she'd stuck around, she probably would be. She hadn't been good at remembering to take her pill, and with the nearest pharmacy an hour away, she proba-bly wouldn't have gotten around to refilling her pre-scription on time. Sooner or later, their protection would have lapsed.

In any case, it had lapsed by now; for several months she hadn't been able to afford her pills.

Not that she and Jake would need protection this week.

"Well," Hank said, "I hope you don't wait too long to start your family."

"Don't worry," Jake said. "We both want a houseful of children. Don't we, darling?"

He'd never called her "darling" until today. She didn't like it, but she smiled anyway, going along with him. "We sure do."

She and Jake certainly hadn't talked about children last summer. They'd been too caught up in the present—and in each other—to plan out the future. It felt odd to do so now.

But if they'd been together the past five months, they would have talked about kids at some point. She turned to Hank. "I was an only child, and so was Jake. It was an easy decision to have more than one."

Hank nodded in approval. "And how many would that be?"

Jake shrugged. "Four, maybe five."

"Five?" Taylor blurted. She quickly recovered and gave a weak smile. "But, Jake, last month you said you'd be happy with three."

He smiled lazily and sipped his wine, looking impossibly sexy. He was too damn good at looking sexy. "Did I?"

"Yes, you did. I remember it clearly," she said, improvising as best she could. "We were, er, decorating the Christmas tree. You looked at the mantel and said we'd be able to hang all five stockings there—one for you, one for me, and three for our three children.''

He adopted a puzzled, tolerant look. ''I thought I said the mantel would fit all five of the *children's* stockings. Ours could go on the bookshelf.''

''That's a mighty big mantel,'' Hank observed. ''I bet you could squeeze in seven if you tried.''

''Good point,'' Jake said. ''See, darling? Anyway, it won't be an issue for another five years, until our last one's born.''

She lifted her chin. ''You expect me to have one baby per year? I don't think so, Jake.''

''Maybe you'll be lucky and get twins,'' Hank suggested helpfully. ''That'd cut down your production time. Melissa's older sisters are twins. Look just like each other.''

''Grandpa...'' Melissa shot Taylor an apologetic look.

The Texan waved a hand in the air. ''A little advice never hurt no one. Anyhow, I'm sure these kids don't mind. They're so crazy in love, nothing bothers 'em. The world could stop spinning and they'd still be staring into each other's eyes. Ain't that right, Jake?''

''That's a fact, Hank. Why, we're practically the perfect couple.''

Taylor wanted to throw up, but did the ladylike thing and changed the subject instead.

When they'd finished dessert, Taylor helped Irma clear the table while Jake led their guests to the living room, where a fire blazed in the hearth.

She met him in the hallway a few minutes later. "I need to talk to you."

He raised an eyebrow. "Oh? Should we tell Hank?"

"Not that kind of talk, Jake." She led him back into the dining room, away from their guests. "A serious talk."

He grinned. "Okay, talk."

From the living room she could hear the two boys playing their favorite smash-'em-up board game while Hank egged them on from the sidelines. She kept her voice low so it wouldn't carry. "Don't you think you're laying it on a bit thick?"

"Hmm?"

"That business about us being *so* great together, all that drivel. Hank's not an idiot, Jake. 'Practically the perfect couple.' Please. What kind of husband would actually say that?"

Jake leaned back against the wall. He slipped his hands into his pockets. "I don't know. A deluded one?"

She glared at him. He was being deliberately maddening. "We're never going to get through the week if you keep this up," she said. "You've got to tone it down. You've made your point—Hank thinks we're crazy about each other. So stop calling me *darling* all the time."

"It suits you."

"And that stuff about having five kids? Give me a break. Five kids." She made a scoffing sound. "I'm not one of your prize heifers."

Jake smothered a grin. "Oh, all right," he said. "Forget the five kids. I can live with three."

She narrowed her eyes. "Very funny."

"Okay, two."

Impatiently, she brushed a lock of hair from her face. Her skin felt flushed, hot. "Look, even if we were still together, I don't do family planning at the dinner table."

He wasn't listening. He was looking at her lips.

"Jake."

They stared at each other for a long moment. Jake was getting too wrapped up in his loving-husband act, but she wasn't going to give in to his teasing.

Then she heard footsteps.

Footsteps coming from the front hall, and Hank's voice. "Hey, Cassidy!" he called. "Where'd you get to? I got a question."

She knew how it would look: husband and wife squared off in the dining room, arguing in whispers. A clear sign of a marriage in trouble.

"Kiss me," Jake said.

Kiss him?

It was the perfect way to hide their argument from Hank, to make sure he didn't guess the truth. And where was the harm in it? She'd been wanting to kiss him ever since he'd walked into the Pancake Hut.

It wouldn't mean anything, she told herself, and it wouldn't change how she felt.

Anyway, there was too much at stake to chicken out now. The Cassidy Ranch needed that grazing land, and she needed Jake's money. She didn't really have a choice.

With half a step she closed the distance between them, pressed her body up against his, tangled her fingers in his short dark hair, and kissed her husband full on the mouth.

Chapter Five

Taylor.

She was in his arms again. All of her. Hot and sexy, with her breasts pressing against his chest and her fingers skimming over his head, flexing and releasing as they tunneled through his hair.

He wasn't ready for her.

Oh, he was *ready* for her, ready to carry her off to his bedroom and ravish her until the sun came up and then to start again at the beginning so they could make love until night fell once more. He felt a powerful, animal need to seduce her, to claim her as his wife in the most elemental way.

One of her legs, he realized, was wrapped around his. He felt the length of her inner thigh—a horse-woman's thigh, long and lean from all the riding she'd done as a teenager at her precious Hunt Club—against the outside of his. And he felt his own arousal leaping in response, pushing insistently against her soft stomach.

His tongue dueled with hers, and now he was the one who pulled her against him. One hand cupped the small of her back, another her rear. She stroked her hand through his hair, inflaming him. Her body pressed rhythmically against his. He felt her nipples brush against his chest, and the sensation almost sent him over the edge.

Almost.

Sanity returned quickly as he once again heard the footsteps approaching through the front hall. It felt like he'd been kissing her for hours, when it had only been seconds. A few passionate seconds.

She'd always had this kind of power over him. She could reduce him to a state of desperate desire in an instant, make him want to throw all caution to the wind and all his promises out the window. He was clay in her hands—her soft, deceptively strong hands.

And they were about to be interrupted in the middle of an X-rated kiss. He broke his lips free from hers. "Taylor, we have to stop."

"Mmm, Jake." She pulled his head back down to hers and connected their lips again. She lifted her body against his and slowly let it slide back down, stroking the entire length of him.

They had to stop. Jake tried to disentangle himself, to peel her arms from around his torso, but it was too late.

Much too late. Hankins turned the corner, calling out, "Jake, Taylor?" He stopped in his tracks as soon as he saw them leaning up against the dining room wall. His jaw dropped, and then he gave a strangled laugh that soon became a full-bodied chortle.

Taylor pulled a few inches away. Her hand loosened its grip on the back of his head, but her other hand stayed where it was, resting on his waist.

Their gazes met, and if Jake hadn't already been blown away, he would have been by the look in her eyes. Kissing her was one thing. Feeling her breasts and her legs against him was another, more glorious thing, but nothing compared to the feeling he got when he looked into her softly passionate hazel eyes. Her pupils were wide, her expression trusting and transported. Flecks of golden color swam in her eyes, which seemed focused only on him, unseeing of everything else.

It was the spark of humor, though, that did him in. The laughter that made her eyes shine, that all but said, "Uh-oh, caught again."

It took him right back to last summer, to the way they'd used to laugh together, making their own little world. This was why he'd fallen in love with her. She might be a spoiled little princess, but she'd been *his* spoiled little princess.

Her capacity for joy in the craziest things had made his heart pound. From the very first time they'd met on the beach, even in the grip of that flash of mutual desire and fascination, he'd felt as if she might burst into delighted laughter just for the joy of being alive.

Now, though, he saw the light fade quickly from Taylor's eyes as she came down to earth, as she realized their kiss had gotten out of control. They'd both forgotten it was only an act. He'd been so damn glad to have her in his arms again that he'd forgotten all about Hank and his grandkids, about Irma and the approaching storm. He'd forgotten the past five months of living alone in this big house, of working his tail off every single day and well into every night, only daring to go to bed when he knew he was too tired to stay up pining after his debutante wife.

Taylor unwrapped her leg from around his, the last sliding contact making him jump once again.

How embarrassing, he thought, to get so carried away by a simple kiss that he'd lost track of his goals. The only reason Taylor was here was so he could get the land he needed. He couldn't set himself up for more heartache by forgetting himself.

If he kissed her again it would be with one purpose only—to prove to Hank that they were still married, still madly in love. He wouldn't let this happen again.

"Well, well, well," said Hankins, "what have we here? Two little lovebirds, maybe?"

Jake felt caught, exposed. Angry. It wasn't supposed to be this way, not at all. Hank was supposed to see a farce, a lie. That he'd seen even a shred of the truth, the truth that Jake still wanted his wife with a passion that could blow the top off a volcano, made him feel unexpectedly vulnerable.

And there was another thing he was going to expose, he realized as Taylor tried to move away from him. Despite being caught in the act, his desire hadn't abated.

Reaching out, he took Taylor by the waist and dragged her swiftly and possessively back against him. She faced away from him this time, and he felt her give a little jump as they touched, as she felt him pressing against the soft curve of her rear end.

She was an effective shield, but she wasn't going to do anything to make the problem go away. And that was just too bad. He draped his arms around her, linking his hands across her stomach like a loving husband would, and forced himself to smile at Hank over her head. "Hello, Hank," he said.

"Hello yourself, loverboy," Hank returned, chortling again.

Taylor wriggled, trying to get a little distance between them, but it only made her move against him and threw him back into his raw needs again. Carrying on a conversation was going to be difficult. Especially when he had a strong urge to bop Hank on the nose, turn Taylor around and start kissing her again.

"I got a question," Hank said. "I want to go see my land one more time before I give it up forever. With this storm coming in like you say it might, I figure I hain't gonna have another chance after tomorrow. Thought I might borrow one of your horses and ride out. What do ya think?"

If Jake understood the man, he wasn't so much asking for permission as telling Jake what he'd be doing the next day. He couldn't really say no, and there wasn't any reason why he would, except to make sure Hank didn't get into trouble if the storm came on early. "I'll go with you," he told his guest.

"Will ya now? That's a great idea. Taylor, you can come along, too. We'll make an outing of it. Heck, we could even bring along the kids. Make it a real family picnic."

Taylor craned her head around, silently asking if she should join them. Jake shrugged his response, trying to tell himself he didn't care whether she came or not. But to his frustration, he did. He wanted to ride with her like he had last summer.

His mind flashed to a memorable summer day when he'd been mending fences with Ty a couple miles from the house. He'd been surprised by the sound of approaching hoofbeats, then gut-wrenchingly happy to see his wife ride up over a rise, wearing jeans and a yellow tank top, her short hair flying free in the wind.

She hadn't given him a chance to say no. She'd slid forward on the western saddle and kicked her boots free of the stirrups. Without a word he'd mounted up behind her. He'd reached for the reins and urged his big bay mare into a fast gallop toward a line shack half a mile away.

At the line shack he'd leaped down from the mare before picking Taylor up and pulling her down against him. Her tank top ripped as he'd pulled it off her. Then they were inside the line shack, tumbling onto the small bed, discovering again their own slice of heaven.

He'd come back to his senses with Taylor in his

arms and the line shack looking like a tornado had hit it. Boots were everywhere. His jeans were halfway to the old potbellied stove, and his shirt had flown back out the still-open door.

They were made for each other, their passion absolutely perfect. Matched strength for strength, desire for desire. She'd drowsed in his arms, a smile of contentment on her sexy face.

Her own top was ruined, so he'd given her his denim shirt, and had ridden back toward the break in the fence bare-chested, sending Taylor home alone when they were still one ridge away from the break so they could maintain at least some semblance of privacy.

The remembered afternoon faded with a jolt as he realized Hank was talking. "Well, I'm glad you want to come along, Taylor. That's mighty good of you..."

She was coming. They were going riding together. He wondered if the memories were as strong for her as they were for him, or if she'd put those things behind her.

"Especially since that way you and your loving husband won't have to be apart for long. And I know how you hate to be apart. Wouldn't want to be the person who kept you from each other. No siree!"

Good old Hank. Well, if he only knew how good they'd gotten at spending time apart, he wouldn't be worried. Five months. Five long months in which they hadn't talked, hadn't touched, hadn't done anything but think about each other and try to figure out what the hell had gone wrong.

Well, he'd thought about her. Heaven only knew if she'd spared him even a moment's consideration after she'd left him eating her dust that day. She might not have, and that was a good reminder.

He was in too deep with her. Way too deep. She made him want things he couldn't have, made him depend on things he couldn't depend on. She'd left him once, despite their mutual passion, and she would leave him again at the end of the week, just as they'd agreed. He couldn't lose his head.

He had to stop thinking about her as his lover and remember she was just his wife.

"Looking forward to it, Hank," he said.

Looking forward to the fact that it was cold outside so Taylor would be wearing a heavy coat that would cover her delectable rear end, and thick pants that would disguise the shapely length of her legs. He hoped. Otherwise he was in serious danger of sending Hank back alone and taking his wife off to another isolated line shack so they could straighten a few things out. "But let's leave the kids at home," he suggested. "I don't want to risk having them out there with that front coming in, even if it passes us by."

"Good enough," Hank said. "You two get back to what you were doing, okay?" he added with a chuckle. "Didn't mean to disturb you or anything."

He left, and they were alone again in the dining room. They stayed as they were for a long moment, not moving, hardly breathing.

Jake savored the sensation, the feeling of contact between them. Desire wasn't the foremost thing in his mind at the moment, much to his surprise. Instead it was just the feeling of their bodies touching, the sense of connection it gave him.

He'd missed her. God, but he'd missed her these past few months.

The fact that he'd also hated her didn't really make a difference. That he'd been happy not to hear her complain about how much time he spent working on the ranch, how he ignored her.

He'd missed the scent of her lingering in the house when he came back from a hard day outside, missed the way he knew what she'd been doing in his absence by the small messes and large disasters she'd left in her wake. Gardening gloves draped haphazardly on the mantelpiece, garden shears and a ring of dirt in the downstairs bathroom sink, a wild profusion of flowers on the nightstand by their bed. Books open on chair arms, stacks of magazines spread across the rugs. A bottle of nail polish on the kitchen windowsill.

She was walking chaos. A never-ending stream of discarded items left behind in her wake, all of it cleaned up by Irma. He suspected he didn't see half of the messes she made in a day.

Despite all that, he'd missed her. Her presence in the house had been inescapable and dynamic. No one could doubt there was a woman living in the Cassidy house at long last, filling it with her smells, her hummed songs, even her periodic tantrums. He missed sharing meals with her, missed wanting her every time he saw her. Missed the sound of her laughter.

She slowly pulled away from him, and he let her. Turning, she faced him from a foot away, still close, still his—even though she wasn't.

"Jake," she said, her voice solemn, soft.

He didn't know what to say, didn't know what she wanted, so he just said, "I know," and kept watching her.

"Jake," she said again, more uncertain now.

He reached out and squeezed her shoulder, trying to make his touch gentle and soothing. "We'll talk later, okay? For now let's go join the others."

Taylor nodded, then padded out of the dining room in front of him.

Frankie and Billy were still in the midst of their smash-'em-up game on the rug, and Melissa sat by herself on the love seat reading a dog-eared soccer magazine she'd brought with her.

Taylor went over to the love seat and sat down next to Melissa. The brown leather was soft and comfortable, warm from the nearby fire. She relaxed back into it, trying not to notice Jake as he moved around the room for several minutes before settling down in a chair close to the hearth to stare moodily into the flames.

Leaning over, she asked Melissa what she was reading, and joined her in a quiet conversation about her high school soccer team. After a while the girl made Billy and Frankie clean up their game and took them off to bed.

Hank was asleep in his armchair, his head thrown back and soft snores coming from the back of his throat. Taylor dared a glance at her husband and found him watching her now, not the fire. There was lazy interest in his eyes, and it brought a warm, flushed feeling to her skin. It wasn't predatory or obviously sexual, but something about it got to her. She felt as if he'd observed her the whole time she'd sat next to Melissa. Watched her the way she used to watch her kitten sleep when she was twelve, fascinated that something could be so sweet and wonderful.

But that was just her imagination. Jake didn't think she was sweet and wonderful. He didn't think she was an adorable kitten who needed love and companionship, but some kind of hellcat who would scratch his eyes out if he gave her the chance.

However much he desired her, he didn't love her, and she had better remember that.

In the fireplace a log settled deeper into the embers, throwing up a shower of sparks. Hank snored one last time, his nostrils rattling, then jerked himself awake, staring around in confusion before shaking his head to clear it.

He gave a little grimace and got to his feet. "Irma's fault," he muttered. "Too much good food." He toddled toward the stairs. "See you both in the morning."

The fire blazed briefly before settling back down to

a few licks of flame on top of orange coals. It gave off a quiet, intense heat, slow and steady.

So different from her marriage, Taylor thought. Her marriage had been like a propane torch, the kind she'd seen Jake use last summer to repair one of the machines for harvesting hay. All noisy passion and anger and all too easily shut off with the twist of a valve.

She was the one who'd done it. She'd wrenched that valve closed and extinguished their marriage utterly and completely.

She turned away as she felt her eyes fill with tears. She'd wanted to be happy, to have all the love and joy that Jake had promised her that week they'd met. He'd seemed so different, so unlike her parents, that she'd blindly trusted her physical intuition and given herself totally to him.

She hadn't held anything back. Okay, so maybe there hadn't been that much depth in her to give. Maybe she'd been nothing more than a spoiled debutante, but she'd put her whole childish, petulant self on a silver platter and handed herself to him. And he'd ignored her. He'd been her parents all over again.

"Taylor?" Jake's voice from across the room, and then again from right behind her. "Taylor?"

She felt the cushions sink as he joined her on the love seat. His hand touched her shoulder, curling softly around it. A tear fell, and then another, sliding down her cheek before dropping to the rug behind the love seat.

She bit back a sob. Somehow she got herself to

stop crying. She closed her eyes and took deep breaths and let herself be aware of Jake behind her on the couch.

He turned her finally, caressing her shoulder with one hand as he brought her around with the other. He stared at her, his gaze moving from her eyes to the streaks of dried tears on her cheeks. "Taylor," he almost groaned. "Oh, God, Taylor. You've been crying."

The urge to bury herself against him and cry her heart out was almost too much to resist. Almost.

She wiped her cheeks with the back of her hand. "I can't handle this, Jake."

One tear squeezed out, but Jake brushed it away with the pad of his thumb before it could trace its way down her face. He pushed her hair back from her eyes, tucking it behind her ear. "What's wrong?" he whispered. "Tell me what's wrong."

What could she say? That she wanted a real marriage? That she wanted a husband who loved her for her flawed self, who cared for her despite who she'd been? Jake obviously wasn't that person, so there was no point burdening him with her foolish needs.

"I didn't want our marriage to fail, Jake." Her throat felt tight. "I've had a hard time these last months and I'm tired. Really tired. More tired than I ever thought possible. Being here brings everything back. All the things that went wrong, all the mistakes we made."

Jake was silent, watching her with compassion.

"I never should have married you, Jake." She gave

a choked laugh. "I should have just had an affair with you and left it at that."

Even voicing that thought made her feel empty inside, as if something were missing.

But an affair with him would have been perfect. A few days of bliss and then she would have gone back to her old life in Boston, still single, still open to the world and excited about new experiences.

Who was she kidding? An affair with Jake would have left her just as wrecked as her marriage had. She wasn't the type to walk away with fond memories and a promise to exchange Christmas cards. Jake was in her blood from the moment she'd seen him on the beach. She would have changed her mind. She would have wanted to spend her life with him. She would have made the same mistake.

"I guess I don't mean that," she admitted, then fell silent again. She turned to stare into the embers of the fire.

"Why didn't you divorce me?" Jake asked after a long silence. His voice was soft, with just that hint of whiskey-roughness, barely more than a whisper.

She didn't know what to say. "I didn't have the money."

He didn't ask the question again, but they both knew that if she'd really wanted a divorce, she could have initiated the proceedings immediately, when she'd still had plenty of her father's money.

But she hadn't. "I—I guess I didn't want to admit how wrong I'd been," she confessed. "I'd made all these plans to spend my life with you and then they disappeared in a puff of smoke.''

Jake touched her shoulder, then traced the length of her arm. ''Would you have done it when you'd saved up the money?''

''I don't know.'' It was the truest answer she could give. Admitting her mistake by filing for divorce would have been wrenching. But there'd been times during the intervening months when she'd been sure she'd wanted one. Sometimes, weak as it was, she'd wished Jake had come after her, fought for her, proved that she was more important to him than his ranch. And she'd wanted to divorce him because he hadn't.

Other times she hadn't thought about it much, though she'd always assumed they'd get divorced eventually.

Jake stood and paced over to the fire. When he spoke he sounded resigned, almost unhappy. ''I've already promised to give you a divorce when this is all over.''

Yes, she thought, but would she still want one?

Chapter Six

At six the next morning, Jake tossed aside the suffocating warmth of his sleeping bag. He stuffed the bag into the closet and rolled up his foam mat, feeling as if he hadn't slept a wink all night. He'd watched the numbers on the digital clock change, had listened to Taylor's deep, even breathing...

How could she possibly sleep with everything that was going on between them? Back in the same house, the same bedroom, the same marriage.

He steeled himself against that line of thought. Time to go to work, he told himself. Time to get some distance, to get his perspective back.

Jake dressed quickly in his long johns and jeans, then came back and sat on the edge of his bed, watching Taylor sleep. She was on her back, one arm over her head.

He couldn't help it. Despite his need for self-protection, his need to get distance, tenderness for her assailed him. She looked so peaceful, so *happy*, lying there with her features soft and her hair spread out in a halo around her head. It was almost like last summer...

Almost. Except back then he'd watched her sleep and he'd wondered if she'd still be around by the time he came home for lunch, or if she'd have left him to go back to the city. He'd surrendered to the inevitability of it, even though he hadn't stopped wanting it to be different.

This time he knew she was leaving. He'd bought her airline ticket. Though the feeling of control was oddly comforting, he still felt that awful emptiness gnawing inside him.

Impulsively he touched her on the shoulder, saying her name. She stirred, then blinked sleepily up at him. For the tiniest fraction of a second he saw desire spring to life in her eyes, memories of the mornings they spent in each other's arms, but then, in another blink, that was gone, replaced by wariness.

"It's okay," he said. She slowly sat up, pulling the sheets up, even though her nightshirt covered everything already. "We never made plans for our trip to see Hank's land."

She nodded. "What time do you want to start out?"

"As soon as Hank finishes his breakfast. We need to get over there and back so I can work this afternoon. It'd be faster just to drive over there in a truck, but I know Hank wants to see his land the old-fashioned way.''

''And you woke me up because...''

''Because I need you to keep him moving. You know how long he took over breakfast yesterday.''

''Yeah, I remember.''

''Good. I'll see you in a couple of hours, then.''

''Set the alarm for seven before you go.''

''How about six-thirty, so you have time for a shower?''

''Seven.''

Turning his back on her, he set the clock for six forty-five and went out to have breakfast with his ranch hands.

Taylor rode out with Jake and Hank after breakfast. She'd dressed for the cold, wearing long johns, jeans and a pair of windproof pants, along with a sweater and her thick down parka.

They went out the main road for a few hundred yards before turning west over a barely discernable track that led back into a valley and then up and over the ridge. Small clouds of vapor escaped from the horses' nostrils as the three made their way across the snowy landscape. The sun poked out from between the clouds every once in a while, and they talked a little as they rode.

Down the other side of the ridge they wound through the trees and out again into open land. There weren't any cattle around. Jake explained to her that they'd brought all the animals close in yesterday in preparation for the storm.

Half an hour later they came to Hank's cabin, nestled against the side of a wooded hill. It looked out on a wide meadow overhung by tall peaks. An old barn sat near the house, and part of the meadow was fenced off into corrals.

Taylor didn't know much about ranching, but the land stretching in front of her was beautiful if nothing else. She imagined in late spring it would be covered with lush grass and a riot of wildflowers.

"Some of the best grazing land around," Hank said proudly as he pulled his horse to a halt and leaned forward on the pommel of his saddle.

"Can't argue with that," Jake said.

Taylor kept silent. The cold was all-pervasive despite her warm layers. Sitting on top of a slow-moving horse didn't exactly get her blood pumping the way a reckless gallop did.

She glanced back up at the ridge of mountains high over them in the distance. As she watched, the gray sky seemed to solidify into a bank of heavy clouds moving steadily eastward. The sun, she realized, hadn't broken out in the past fifteen minutes.

She caught Jake's attention and motioned toward the clouds. He took one look and turned his horse around. "Come on," he said. "Time to head back before we get caught out here."

They rode home at a slightly faster pace than before, not stopping to look at any scenery, but even so it was snowing gently by the time they reached the barn. The wind was picking up and it carried the snow with it.

She saw two of the hands on horseback moving among the cattle in the huge winter pasture. Another of the hands, Linda, drove off somewhere toward the interior of the ranch in one of the ranch's trucks.

The foreman, Stan, came out to greet them as they walked their horses into the barn. "Jake, I need to see you for a minute."

Jake glanced over at Taylor, as if he wondered who would take care of *her* if he had to take care of business. It stung. Had she really been so self-centered last summer that Jake didn't trust her to pull her own weight in a storm?

"I'll take care of the horses." Her voice came out crisp, but she didn't care.

Jake looked surprised, then nodded his approval. He turned to Hank. "Why don't you head back to the house and get warm? Make sure your grandkids are okay. You can let them know we're in for a pretty big storm, so if they want to watch any TV they'd better do it now. The power could go out."

Hank gave his reins over to Taylor and clapped his hands together. He seemed a little embarrassed. "Too much Texas living," he said. "It's thinned my blood."

She and Jake led the horses into tie stalls and then Jake went off to talk with his foreman. Taylor settled down to the pleasurable task of taking care of the horses.

Even a spoiled debutante knew about grooming

horses. One of the few things that had been drummed into her as a young girl was that when you went riding, the first thing you attended to was the comfort of your horse.

Granted, the Hunt Club had a staff of grooms to take care of the pedestrian details of it all, but she could do what needed to be done with her eyes closed.

Removing all the saddles first, she proceeded to groom the animals, and took the liberty of giving each a small measure of grain.

Her tasks done, she looked for Jake but he was nowhere to be found. She put her coat back on and made her way through the thickening snow toward the bulky shape of the calving barn a couple hundred yards away. Inside, Jake stood with Ty, examining a tired-looking cow. She watched them work for a minute, then asked Jake if she should bring in the rest of the horses.

Again he looked surprised, but Taylor decided she'd get used to that eventually. And he would get used to the fact that she wasn't a total waste of a life. Finally Jake nodded. "Yeah. Reid was going to do it, but if you're willing... Watch out for the big paint, though. He's a mean one. Let him stay out in the storm if he's too dumb to come in."

Taylor left the men to doctor the cow and trudged back toward the other barn, where she collected a halter from the tack room and let herself back out into the storm.

Three horses were waiting patiently by the corral

gate, and allowed themselves to be led into stalls without any fuss. The other animals were still in the distance, nothing but dark shapes in the snow. The wind was getting stronger.

She whistled for the horses but the wind whipped the sound away. Stomping out into the long corral, she kept whistling through her cold lips until she was close enough that the horses could hear her. One animal allowed itself to be caught, and most of the others sensed a good thing and followed them back toward the barn.

Inside, she led each horse to a stall and prepared it for the rest of the day and the night, laying out straw and making sure it had hay and water available. She didn't know if she'd done everything just the way Jake and his hands usually did, but she knew the horses were adequately cared for. They'd be fine during the storm—except for the big paint, who hadn't come in.

She went back out into the storm to track him down. That was where Jake found her a few minutes later, staring in frustration at the horse, who'd been evading her best attempts to catch him.

"I thought I told you to leave him outside."

She glared at him from under her snow-covered hood. Blowing snow stung her eyes, and truth be told, she'd been about to leave the animal just at the moment Jake arrived. She shrugged, the gesture lost in the oversize coat. "No harm in trying."

"Yes, there is. You're frozen." He stripped off his glove and touched her cheek. His fingers were warm—hot almost. They seemed to burn into her skin. At the same time his half-tender, half-annoyed expression seemed to bore into her eyes. "Come on back to the barn."

There wasn't anything she could do but comply, so she trudged after him back to the bright warmth of the barn. Inside, the horses filled the space with the noise of loud breaths, clopping hooves, and open-mouthed chewing. Taylor brushed the snow from her jacket. Her face prickled as the circulation came back.

"Where are all the hands?" she asked.

"In the cookhouse, warming up."

"Is everything ready for the storm?"

"Not yet, but I don't believe in working my people until they get frostbite. Let's go over there ourselves. You could use a hot drink."

In the cookhouse the woodstove was going full-blast and the air smelled of damp, sweaty men and women. Everyone had a cup of coffee in their hands—some to drink and others just to hold for the warmth. Orville came up to them as they entered the room and handed them both steaming white mugs.

Taylor felt awkward as they joined the others, not knowing what they thought of her. All of them had been on the ranch five months earlier. They'd seen the passion between Jake and herself, and they'd witnessed her departure. She didn't know how many of them had actually seen her drive off, but if they hadn't seen her they'd at least heard about it. And now she was back. The princess was among them again.

She didn't expect any kind of welcome, but as she

approached the table, Dusty slid aside to give her a length of bench, and Ty waved a good-natured hello. Reid said, "Thanks for taking care of the horses, Taylor," and then the conversation resumed.

Obviously Jake had explained the situation to the satisfaction of his employees.

After a while Stan pushed away his cup and started assigning duties for the next few hours. He didn't give Taylor a task, though. She had to ask Jake what she should do to help out.

He didn't look surprised this time, which was a relief. "The only thing I really need you to do," he said, "is go back to the house and make sure those little hellions don't tear the place down. I want a warm bed to come home to tonight, and I'd hate it if one of them torched the place."

Taylor smiled at the thought of Frankie setting fire to the house. She'd make sure it didn't happen. "Are you going to be back for dinner?"

Jake nodded. "Yeah. We'll get everything straightened away before then. We won't let this weather disrupt us too much. It's just a little extra work right now."

She went out into the storm again, slogging her way across the compound toward the ranch house. Welcoming lights shone out from the windows.

A fire blazed in the living room, and rich smells wafted from the kitchen. Frankie and Billy were glued to the television set in the den, while Melissa read a book on the couch, her expression pained as she tried to block out the noise of the cartoon show.

"Where's Hank?" she asked Irma when she made it into the kitchen. Irma was cleaning up dishes from the lunch she'd served for their guests.

"Resting. He was looking after the boys for a while, and I think it tuckered all three of them out. Gave Melissa a bit of a break, though. Poor girl."

"What can I do?"

Giving no evidence of surprise, Irma looked her over and said, "First you can go get warm. Then come back and eat. You missed lunch. Can't have you running on empty at a time like this." She paused and waved toward a plate on the counter. "Then you can have some of these madeleines and help me get dinner together. There's a few things I want to do around the house before the weather gets any worse. Orville said it's going to drop twenty degrees by nightfall."

Taylor spent the afternoon alternately helping Irma and entertaining their guests. Irma took her help for granted. Taylor relished the feeling of having someone depend on her.

Hank came down midafternoon, ready to head back out into the storm. She directed him over to the cookhouse to check in with Orville, who was supposed to be in radio contact with all the hands. The boys grew bored with the television and had to be coaxed into playing a board game with Melissa.

Jake and Hank showed up just before dinnertime looking wet and cold. Mud coated Jake's jeans and his hands were raw and red, as if he hadn't been wearing his gloves. They both went upstairs to change without saying a word, but when Jake came back down ten minutes later in clean clothes and with his hair neatly combed, he had a smile on his face. "It's good to be warm."

Taylor stood in the hallway with a dish towel in her hand, watching through the open doorway as Jake sat on a couch in the den and started talking with the three children.

She smiled at the scene. Jake was good with the kids, even if he did think they came from a strange alien planet of bad manners.

For the past five months she'd concentrated on seeing Jake only as a man who didn't love her, a man who couldn't see past his ranch to take care of his wife. But obviously he was more than that. If he'd cared for nothing but his ranch, he wouldn't have bothered to come home for dinner, and he certainly wouldn't have bothered to talk with three kids who probably bugged the daylights out of him.

How selfish she'd been, to see only the part of Jake that affected her. She hadn't tried to understand him at all.

She went back into the kitchen to put the finishing touches on the vegetables and then slipped into the dining room to set the table.

Jake joined her. "How was your afternoon?"

"Warmer than yours, it looks like."

He shrugged. "A tree came down across a fence in the winter pasture. Hank and I took care of it."

"So everything's all set for the storm?"

"Looks that way."

But the storm had its own ideas. Halfway through dinner the power went out. It flickered once, then again, then cut off completely, leaving only the candles on the table and the warm orange glow of the fire in the living room to illuminate the house.

Jake pushed back his chair. "I'll go start the generator."

Taylor watched from her seat at the other end of the table as he left the dining room. She heard him putting on his heavy coat and then saw the slicing light of a flashlight cut through the darkness of the front hall. The back door opened, then banged closed.

Taylor looked around the table. Her four guests looked at her expectantly. Billy had a bite of food halfway to his mouth; it seemed stuck there as if held up by invisible strings. He'd obviously forgotten about it.

She felt like an absurd hostess, and suddenly realized she wanted to help Jake, not sit at the dining room table trying to pretend nothing had happened. "I'll be right back." She slipped into her jacket and snow boots before following Jake's path through the back door.

The wind was howling outside. She slogged through the snow over to where Jake stood in the protection of a shelter built against the back of the house. The flashlight was tucked under his arm.

She called out his name and he turned. "What are you doing out here, Taylor? You should be inside, staying warm."

She felt like the recipient of a taped message on

repeat play. "I'm not going to freeze in the next five minutes, Jake. Show me how this thing works."

"You really want to know?"

"Yes." She shook her head at him. "What if I need to turn it on when you're not around?"

He stared at her, then nodded. "Good point. Here's what you do." He showed her where the On switch was located, made her pump fuel into the engine from the attached tank, and showed her how to operate the choke. "Now all you have to do is pull on the rope."

She pulled. There was a lot more resistance than she'd anticipated. The flywheel turned reluctantly and the motor gave a halfhearted chug.

Jake looked as if he wanted to relieve her of her task, but she glared him back. "It was heavier than I thought, that's all," she explained.

She was no wimp. All her life she'd been an athlete, and the past few months of waitressing hadn't done anything to atrophy her muscles. Plates of food were heavy, especially when you carried a lot of them in a busy place like the Pancake Hut. So were bus tubs full of dirty dishes, and immense stock pots full of soapy water. And tall garbage cans full of kitchen refuse. She'd handled it all, and she wasn't about to let a little generator get the better of her.

Bracing herself, she gave the cord a firm yank. This time the flywheel spun easily. The engine caught, roaring to life with a belch of smoke from its exhaust pipe. "Let it run for a second," Jake instructed, "then slowly move the choke lever back to the run position."

She did so. The sound of the engine smoothed out into a low, growling rumble.

"Nicely done, Taylor."

She beamed at his praise, feeling good. "So the lights are back on?"

Jake opened a gray metal box on the wall and flipped a breaker switch. "Now they are. I'll show you how to refill the generator tomorrow, in daylight."

They went back inside. Everything was bright again. As they hung up their coats, Jake said, "Let's turn off all the lights we don't need."

She went upstairs while Jake went into the living room. Aside from the overhead fixture in the hallway, the only light on was in Hank's bedroom. She hadn't been in the room since she'd removed her belongings two days ago. All of Hank's things were neatly put away, though not as neatly as she would have had to keep things if she'd stayed in this room.

She switched off the light, wondering what would have happened if Hank and his grandkids hadn't come to stay. She and Jake might have seen them only once or twice so far.

Without the pressure of sleeping in the same room, she and Jake probably would have done their best to ignore each other. And only being on display for a few minutes at a time would have made their pretense easier.

But she didn't really mind the way things were working out. Sure, it was a little more intense than she'd bargained for, and it brought up all kinds of emotions, but she didn't mind having a second chance with her husband.

She switched off the light and the room fell into darkness. No light came in through the windows. There was nothing to look at outside except the snow blowing against the glass.

A second chance.

Was that what she wanted, really? She looked down at her left hand, at the wedding set she'd worn with such happiness on her wedding day last summer, and which she'd put back on with such ambivalence just two days ago. The diamond on the engagement ring flashed almost imperceptibly, picking up some stray beam of light.

She and Jake were still married. They were still bound together by a higher power than the two of them put together. It wasn't right to give up on that. It certainly wasn't right to give up on it after only five weeks, as she'd done last summer.

Her mind spun as she made her way through the darkened hallway. All those months in Boston she'd been so sure of herself, so convinced she'd done the right thing. Being back in Montana undermined everything, shook everything up.

A second chance.

She had one. She had a chance to make her marriage work, to make up for the mistakes she'd made. She'd thought her mistake was in marrying Jake, but it wasn't. It was in leaving him after only five weeks, without giving them a chance to know each other.

She hadn't destroyed their marriage single-handedly, but she'd been the first to give up, and that was wrong.

Chapter Seven

Slowly Taylor made her way down the stairs, thinking about second chances.

Jake waited for her in the front hall. "You probably have grease on your hands. We should wash up."

Taylor glanced down at her fingers. Two of them were streaked with grease, and when she raised them to her nose she caught the sharp odor of gas. She wrinkled her nose.

Jake smiled at her. "Welcome to life on a ranch. I wish I could say everything always smelled great around here, but that just isn't true."

Taylor smiled back, aware that Jake hadn't been teasing or mocking her, or trying to make her feel like an inferior city girl. She thought of all the smells of the ranch—grease and fuel, the strong smell of the cattle, the clean wind out of the mountains, the fields of grass and wildflowers, fresh-cut alfalfa, clean hay, sweaty horses.

Good and bad, she thought, turning on the water in the downstairs bathroom. And it stacked up pretty well against Boston, where the major smell was the lung-choking odor of rush-hour exhaust and, for her, the smell of greasy food frying on a grill.

At the table, the two boys were just finishing up their meal. Irma whisked the boys' plates away before they got any ideas about playing with the food they hadn't managed to eat.

Jake turned his attention to the kids. "For as long as this storm lasts, I don't want any of you going outside without one of us accompanying you, and none of you leaves the house at night."

The boys nodded solemnly, as did Melissa. Jake asked the two boys if they'd ever been in a storm like this before. When they said no, he said, "This is going to be a bad one, but everything will be okay. If you get scared about anything, you come to one of us, all right?"

"I don't get scared," said Billy.

"Neither do I," his brother echoed.

"Well, I do sometimes," Jake said. "And so does Taylor, and I bet even your grandpa gets a little nervous every once in a while. It's nothing to be ashamed of."

A flicker of relief moved through Frankie's expression. "I don't get scared," he repeated, but not so adamantly.

"Fine," Jake said. "But if you change your mind,

just come and talk to one of us. Now, what do you suppose Irma made for dessert?''

Irma served applesauce, having learned her lesson about feeding too much sugar to heathens too close to bedtime.

Taylor helped Irma clean up from the meal, then went to join the others in the living room.

Jake wasn't there. Nor, she realized, had his coat been hanging on the coat tree in the hallway. ''Where's Jake?'' she asked the room in general.

Hank's only answer was a soft snore. Melissa said, ''The foreman called on the radio. Jake said to tell you he went down to the calving barn. There are a couple of hurt animals. He said he'd be back soon.''

Taylor looked around the living room. Hank slept, the two boys played quietly—as if the storm had sucked some of the excess energy out of them—and Melissa read another sports magazine.

She made a quick decision. Last summer in a situation like this she would have stayed by the fire and curled up under a blanket. She might have even been jealous of the time Jake spent on the animals. But she was different now. If cows were hurt, they needed to be helped. No question about it. And she needed to play her part.

Especially if she was having thoughts of staying married to Jake. A spike of embarrassment shot through her as she remembered her angry words the day she'd stormed off the ranch last summer.

I married you, Jake, not your ranch!

But maybe that was part of the problem. Whether

she liked it or not, staying with him meant being involved in life on the ranch.

"Will you be okay here alone?" she asked Melissa. "I'm going to help out with the animals. Irma's in the kitchen if you need anyone, okay?"

"Sure," Melissa said. "We'll be fine. I'm going to put Frankie and Billy to bed soon anyway."

Taylor left the house ten minutes later, wearing every stitch of warm clothing she owned. Her powerful flashlight cast a murky beam through the storm.

As she approached the calving barn she heard the growl of a big generator under the howling of the wind. She yanked open the big sliding door wide enough to slip inside and closed it quickly behind her. It was warm in the barn, and rich with the scents of tired, wet animals. Jake stood with two others in one of the stalls, looking down at a cow.

"What's wrong with her?" Taylor asked when she got close enough.

Jake swiveled toward her, his expression resigned. "Taylor. Why am I not surprised to see you here?"

"Because you're a quick learner."

"And you're a damned fool." He said it almost affectionately, as if he was happy to see her. "No offense," he added. "But why the dickens won't you stay inside where it's warm?"

She ignored the question. "What can I do?"

"You've been saying that a lot lately."

"Get used to it, Jake. Anyway, it's only for a week."

The moment the words were out of her mouth she

regretted them. She wasn't sure she wanted them to be true. They were a potent reminder that she was only here for one specific purpose.

To fulfill that purpose, she should be back at the house baby-sitting Hank and his grandkids. But she wasn't. She was out here in the cold showing Jake she wasn't the spoiled brat he'd married six months before.

"Look," she said, "there must be something I can do. What about the horses? Has anyone looked in on them recently?"

Jake sighed. "Okay, you can check on the horses. I'll walk you over."

"I can make it on my own."

He looked her up and down. "I know, but it's nighttime and I'd worry about you. Three winters ago in a blizzard like this one, a hand on Frank Hapman's ranch died between the barn and the bunkhouse. It happens."

Taylor swallowed, suddenly feeling a little scared. She hadn't realized she'd been tempting fate by walking a few hundred yards through the blowing snow. She felt very naive about real life on a ranch.

But it couldn't be any harder than scraping out a life in the inner city of Boston, alone except for her pride.

"Uh, I'd love to have you walk me there, Jake."

"Good. Sorry to scare you."

She linked her arm securely through his as they pushed back out into the storm. Together they fired up the generator and turned on the lights. "I'll come back for you in an hour," Jake told her. "Don't leave, and don't do anything foolish."

"Yes, sir," she said jokingly.

"Be careful, Taylor," he said, and then he tilted her face up to his and kissed her briefly on the lips.

She felt the lingering warmth of his lips long after he was gone. The barn was cold, but not bitterly so. She kept her coat on as she moved from stall to stall, stroking and calming the horses. She checked on their supplies of hay and water, and mucked out a couple of stalls that needed it.

She walked through the rest of the barn, looking for any signs of trouble from the storm. She didn't really know what she was looking for, but she did her best anyway.

A bleating noise from the far corner of the barn reminded her of the two goats she'd visited the first morning she was back. She let herself into their stall to check on their situation, and stroked both of them on their bristly coats.

Before she knew it Jake was back, calling her name as the big sliding door rumbled shut. She freed herself from the affectionate animals and made her way to the front of the barn. "Everyone's fine," she called as soon as she saw him across the barn. "Even the goats."

"You still want to help out, or are you ready to go back to the house?"

She felt energized by her last hour with the animals. "What needs to be done?"

"How are your short-order cooking skills?"

"I'm just a waitress, Jake. The closest I got was the dishwashing station."

"Sleazy Steve made you wash dishes?"

Taylor felt herself blush despite the cold. "Yeah. For the first two months. Right after he hired me as a waitress I got demoted for talking back to a customer." She forced a laugh. "It was hell on my manicure."

Jake took off his gloves and reached for her bare hands. He turned them over so he could see each side. "Taylor…"

She shook her head. "Now you're going to smell like goat. Jake, it was no big deal. I didn't understand the rules, but I learned my lesson. Don't tell me you're getting in a twist about it." She forced another laugh. "I'd think it was exactly the kind of thing you thought a spoiled girl like me deserved."

He watched her for a long moment. "I did have thoughts like that. But I didn't want it to really happen."

"It happened. And I'm a better person for it." She wasn't going to belabor the point. "Now, what kind of help does Orville need?"

"Everything you've got. I need him to work outside, but someone's got to keep the food and coffee coming. Usually I get Irma to come down, but I'd just as soon give her a break."

Taylor thought of some of the messes she'd made the summer before, and how Irma had always cleaned up without complaining. "Sure, I'll do my best."

At the cookhouse Orville took a few minutes to

show her the ropes and then joined the others. Taylor didn't bother to ask what they were doing. All she knew was that cold, hungry cowboys and cowgirls were going to come through the doorway, and she was going to bust her butt to have hot coffee and plenty of food waiting for them.

Every fifteen minutes or so for the next four hours someone, or two or three someones, came banging through the cookhouse door, brushing snow off their clothes and grabbing a cup of coffee before sitting bleary-eyed in front of the woodstove that Taylor kept stoked. She cooked whatever anyone asked for and did her best to keep the place clean.

A little after two o'clock in the morning Jake came in for the third time and told her to shut off the stove and come back to the house.

He bundled her into her coat and led her across the snowy ground toward the dark house. She thought the wind had died down somewhat and said as much to Jake, who nodded. "Yeah, things have eased in the last couple of hours. We're not through it yet, but we'll worry about it in the morning."

The house was quiet except for the muffled sound of the generator out back. The only light came from the fixture in the front hall. "Normally I'd shut down the generator at this time of night," Jake said, "but with guests in the house the extra gas is worth it."

"What about the water heater?" Taylor asked, her voice a whisper as they went upstairs.

"The appliances run on propane. Take as long a shower as you want."

She glanced over at Jake, who'd been out in the cold all night while she'd been safe in the warmth of the cookhouse. "You first."

He gave her hand a squeeze. "Thanks. Not that I wouldn't have been a gentleman about it, but... Well, as it is, I'm probably going to fall asleep standing up in the shower."

They were inside their bedroom now, with the door closed. "Get going," she said.

She went to the window while he showered, looking out into the darkness of the storm, seeing into herself as much as out the window. Jake was a good man. A hardworking man. She hadn't been able to see that last summer, but she could now.

When the bathroom was free she stumbled into the shower and washed herself on autopilot, loving the feel of the warm water sluicing over her body.

She got out, dried herself off in the steamy air and slipped into her nightshirt. The bedroom was dark, but just before she turned out the bathroom light she saw the unmistakable sight of Jake's large body taking up most of their bed.

He'd probably been too tired to lay out his sleeping bag, or too exhausted to face a night on the hard floor. She was too exhausted to care. She closed the bathroom door behind herself and slipped into bed beside her husband.

He didn't move. His body was already soft with sleep, and it gave off a wonderful heat. She snuggled up close and was asleep within seconds.

* * *

Comfort.

Warmth.

Deep contentment.

Even half conscious, Jake knew something was totally right in the world. Something was absolutely, perfectly wonderful.

He stretched his aching limbs and pulled Taylor more tightly against him. He luxuriated in the soft heat of her body, spooned against his from head to foot. Her hair tickled his nose. With every breath he inhaled the clean, sexy scent of her skin. He could feel her heartbeat marking time with his own, measuring out the slow, steady drumbeat of sleep.

Slowly his eyes opened. He stared over at the digital clock on the nightstand. Its red numbers glowed five forty-five and were the only illumination in the room.

He blinked once, then again. He raised his head, suddenly aware of Taylor lying next to him in his bed. The light from the clock washed over her face.

She made a little noise, a sleepy moan, barely audible, and wriggled back against him. He felt himself come fully awake, and fully alive, as he realized what was going on.

He and Taylor were in the same bed. Touching each other. Two thin scraps of cotton and silk away from being naked, from making love.

To his surprise, though, his main instinct was to lie down and try to go back to sleep. Something about the intimacy of sleeping in each other's arms again aroused a whole different part of his being. He felt the most incredible sense of tenderness toward Taylor, the strangest urge to hold her and protect her and keep her warm forever.

It was worse than just wanting her. Sexual urges he could handle, but this new fierce protectiveness was a problem. It reminded him too much of the way he'd felt when he'd first brought Taylor back to the ranch. The same out-of-control sensation that had made him work so hard on the ranch, trying to stop himself from getting too close to her.

Then it had been more simple, though. His return to the ranch with his bride had underscored for him how foolishly he'd thrown himself into marriage.

With his history, though, it wasn't possible to get into marriage any other way. Marriage and Cassidy men didn't agree. Not that he'd ever witnessed one in action. His grandmother had died giving birth to his father, and from what he'd heard her marriage had not been a smooth one. His mother had left when he was a newborn, eager to get free of the ranch. She hadn't wanted to take Jake with her, perhaps because he was tainted with ranching blood and would always be a reminder of her marriage.

Any thinking man with that history wouldn't want to risk getting married. But Jake hadn't been thinking when he'd married Taylor. Not with his brain, anyway. She'd seemed too good to be true. A goddess made flesh. A woman he desired like no other, who made his every fantasy come true. Who made him throw caution to the wind.

Like a fool. Like a sick, love-struck fool.

When the smoke cleared he realized he'd married another city girl who wouldn't be able to tolerate life on the ranch. He'd known from the moment he arrived with her in the cab of his truck that she wouldn't be staying for the rest of her life, like she'd promised. She'd get sick of it, and she'd leave, just like his mother.

She had, too. Not even the passion that raged between them had been enough to keep the inevitable from happening.

But this, he thought, holding Taylor's sleeping body in his arms, was something different. This wasn't desperation that held them together, but something far more powerful.

Taylor stirred again and opened her eyes. She twisted to face him. Her expression was trusting, calm. She touched the whole length of him with her body, and he couldn't do anything but pull her close against him and hold her tight. His desire settled against her stomach, pressing. She gave a small noise from the back of her throat and buried her lips against his neck.

Last summer, Jake thought, he would have been inside her already. But this morning he was still too firmly in the grip of that languorous feeling of caring.

Not for long, though, if she kept moving her body against his.

"Taylor," he said softly, with the barest hint of warning in his voice. "Taylor, wake up."

Silence. Then she murmured, "Too tired to wake

up,'' and moved against him again, a small, womanly movement that started him down the slippery slope to total loss of control.

He moved himself backward on the bed, just out of range. "Taylor, you've got to wake up. We're in bed together."

"Mmm."

He took a deep breath to steady his nerves. "Taylor, if you don't wake up right now, I'm going to be inside you within about thirty seconds, and I'm going to make love to you until you scream loud enough to turn the power back on."

Another sigh. "Mmm." Then a caught breath, a twitch, and a gasp. "Oh, my God!" Taylor whipped away from him, moving swiftly up the bed to sit against the headboard, the sheets pulled up to her neck. "Jake!"

He successfully fought the urge to burst out laughing, but couldn't restrain his smile. "Good morning, Taylor." God but she was beautiful when she was flustered.

"Uh, hi. Good morning."

"Sleep well?" he asked her.

She colored. "Uh…"

"I did."

"Jake, tell me we didn't…"

"We didn't."

She closed her eyes. He watched her take a deep breath and slowly let it out. She was so gorgeous. "I only said that to wake you up. You…had your own ideas about how you wanted to start the day."

"Oh."

"Believe me," he said, "the feeling was mutual.
But when we make love it has to be because we both
want it, not because we let our bodies get too close."

She swallowed. *"When?"*

"Hmm?"

"You said *when,* not if. *When* we make love."

Had he? If so, he was farther over the edge than
he thought. But he wasn't going to take it back. "I
want to make love with you, Taylor. It wouldn't be
smart, but I can't help wanting it."

"I can't talk about this, Jake."

"I'm not trying to pressure you. Just telling the
truth. But if I couldn't ever make love to you again,
and instead could wake up with you in my arms every
day, I'd take that bargain in a second."

Something in her face seemed to melt. "Jake..."

He had to get out of this bed. Now. This business
of baring his soul first thing in the morning was way
too strange. "It's not sweet talk, Taylor," he murmured as he peeled back the bedclothes and stood.
He crossed to the bathroom. "I've missed you," he
said, and closed the bathroom door before he could
say anything else he might regret.

Chapter Eight

I've missed you.

Those words echoed in Taylor's brain all day long as she worked around the house and the ranch. They echoed in her mind and in her body and in her whole consciousness.

This morning they'd seemed to be wrenched out of Jake, a confession he didn't want to give, and he hadn't referred to their brief interlude any time they saw each other.

Had Jake really meant it? Had he missed her in anything but the most physical way? And why hadn't he taken advantage of her sleepy state to seduce her that morning?

She didn't know how to think about it. Last summer they'd never passed up an opportunity to make love.

Of course, then they'd been married, not separated.

Not for the first time, Taylor wondered if she could even compare her current relationship with Jake to her old one. The only constant thing was their physical desire, and aside from that it was like she was seeing him—really seeing him—for the first time. Learning about him. Watching him, instead of being wrapped up only in herself.

That day she spent more time with the horses, and more time in the cookhouse keeping everyone warm and fed and caffeinated.

The storm was less frightening during the day. The wind had died down a bit and the thickly falling snow was like something out of a Norman Rockwell painting. It blanketed the earth in perpetual newness, erased footsteps and vehicle tracks almost as soon as they were made. Even the snowplows hooked to the front of the ranch trucks couldn't make a lasting dent.

The weather seemed to forgive everything. It wiped away all mistakes, provided a clean slate.

The radio in the cookhouse was on nonstop. The weather reports predicted that the worst of the storm would be over by midnight. The power lines to the ranch would be back up within a matter of days, and the dangerous period for the animals would be past.

Taylor took off from her duties to eat dinner with Hank and the kids. Jake didn't join them. As soon as the meal ended she returned to the cookhouse.

At eleven that night the snow stopped. At twelve-thirty a slice of moon broke through the previously impenetrable cloud cover and cast its white clear light over the snowy ground, sparkling in the few remaining snowflakes. Most of the hands were at the cook-house, and everyone tumbled outside into the cold to stare up into the sky at the moon and stars.

Taylor felt a deep connection to the people who worked on Jake's ranch. Other storms would come through before the winter was over, but they'd worked together and gotten through this one with only a single cow lost.

Jake sent everyone home for the night. "Sleep," he told them. "We'll clean this place up in the morning."

Everyone wandered off, until it was just Jake and Taylor standing in the cold clear air outside the cook-house. He put his arm around Taylor's shoulders. "Thank you. Thank you for all your help."

They went back in and shut everything down for the night, then walked across the snow-covered compound with their arms linked, even though there was no danger that the storm would whip one of them away. Still, the contact felt good. If there was a bond between herself and the other hands after weathering the storm, there was even more of a bond growing between herself and Jake.

Nothing like this had taken place last summer. Taylor couldn't remember an instance when she'd left the ranch house at any time of the day or night for any reason other than her own personal pleasure.

It had always been about what she wanted, not what needed to be done.

She thought she'd learned a lot during the past few months, but being back on the ranch had taught her even more. Her experience of being down and out had taught her to take care of herself. On the ranch, though, it wasn't herself that needed looking after. It was the cattle who were at risk, her guests whose safety and happiness were her concern. Her husband with whom she had to learn to interact.

Her husband.

Together they stepped up onto the porch. Taylor turned to look out over the ranch. She brushed her hood back from her head so she could see everything.

The moon disappeared behind a cloud and the snowy world was bathed in dim, diffused light. Then the cloud passed and the moonlight struck the ground again, illuminating first the sweeping expanse of the winter pasture, then the various buildings that made up the ranch.

In the black sky the stars were almost hidden by the bright moon. She felt Jake's hand on her shoulder, and wondered how long it had been there. The clouds of vapor from their breaths rose and mingled in front of them.

Slowly, just to test how it felt, she leaned her body a little bit against Jake. She felt a flowing warmth begin at the area where they touched. It seeped into the nearby flesh, making her side feel soft and languid. She felt as if he were a magnet pulling her inexorably toward him.

Her head rested against the cool leather shoulder of his sheepskin coat, and she marveled at the feeling that swamped her body. Not lust. Not desire. But trust.

Trust.

How could she never have felt this before? She'd lived with the man for five weeks as his wife. She'd been around him as constantly as he would allow her, and yet she'd never felt this peaceful sense of trust before. Just being together. Just standing together. Without tearing each other's clothes off, without kissing each other, without trying to devour each other and conquer each other in passion.

Was that how it had been between them? she wondered. A contest? A competition?

What would it be like to make love to her husband without being blinded by lust? To savor every moment instead of pushing toward culmination? She'd thought sex between them was good before, but it would be fantastic if they ever made love again. She shivered just thinking about it.

"Cold?"

No, she wasn't cold. "I'm fine," she said, aware that her voice seemed to come out an octave lower than usual.

Jake gave her shoulder a small squeeze and said, "Well, I hate to admit it, but I am. Let's go in and get some sleep."

They went upstairs to the dark second floor. The generator, which Taylor had learned how to refuel that afternoon, was still going strong. She turned on the light on the nightstand and they both looked at the empty bed.

The moment stretched out. She wondered what he was thinking, what he wanted. She wanted exactly what they'd had last night, to drowse in his arms and wake up feeling wonderful.

She swiveled her face to meet his gaze. There was a softness in his eyes that affected her like gentle breath on a bed of coals. She felt herself glow a little, felt the blood come to her skin all over her body. She knew she radiated heat and warmth.

"We could sleep together," Jake offered. "Like last night."

She drew in a slow, deep breath, allowing his words to create a vivid picture in her mind. She could almost feel the length of him snuggled close against her back, his arms around her, his breath tickling her ear, his legs tangled with hers, his desire pressing...

His desire pressing against her, making her want more.

"Jake," she said, "we're tired, but we're not as tired as we were last night."

"Nothing has to happen."

She took another deep breath. "You might have that much self-control, Jake, but I don't. When we make love I—"

"When?"

She closed her eyes. "If. If we make love."

"If we make love, what?"

"I don't know." She couldn't remember what she'd been about to say. "I want to sleep next to you, but I don't think it's a good idea."

He nodded slowly. "I know."

She smiled up at him, feeling suddenly brave. "Not that I don't want to make love to you, Jake."

He smiled back at her. "Careful, Taylor."

"It's just the truth, Jake. You're a good man, and you're sexy as all get-out. It's impossible not to want you."

"Taylor…"

She broke eye contact, turning away from him. She took two steps toward the bathroom, opened the door, and walked in. Over her shoulder she said, "I just want it to be special," then closed the door and turned the bolt to lock it.

Jake stood there for a full minute, not moving. He felt the blood pounding in his body, felt his heart beating faster than it had a right to.

Sex. It was always there between them, threatening to take up all the available space in their relationship. How easy it would be for sex to be the only thing that held them together, just as it had been in the summer. But that had been a complete disaster. If he wanted anything to be different in the future, he would have to rethink a lot of his old assumptions.

When had he started thinking about the future? The future with Taylor, rather than without her? And when had she started to think of a future with him?

When we make love.

They'd both said it.

It was hard to wrap his mind around the idea of a future with Taylor, hard to know if he wanted it. She'd left him once already, and it would be hard to believe in her again. But she'd changed a lot since the summer. She wasn't the same person.

No kidding.

Last summer she'd never helped out around the ranch. Her presence in the house had been inescapable, but the ranch had been his and his alone. His space to get away from her, to make sure she didn't take over every waking and sleeping moment of his life. To protect himself from her inevitable departure.

Now she was underfoot all day long. He loved it, and he hated it. They got along well, but it wouldn't work in the long term. He couldn't survive if they were joined at the hip.

Then again, he didn't know how much longer he would survive if they weren't.

Jake broke himself free of his frozen state and went to the closet for his sleeping pad and bag.

After only a few minutes, Taylor came out of the bathroom in a cloud of steam. She had a towel wrapped around herself and another turbaned around her head. She carried her clothes in her hands. Jake couldn't stop himself from imagining what would happen out here when he went into the shower. Taylor would unwrap the towel from around her head and run her fingers through her still-damp hair, then peel away her towel. She'd slowly dress herself in her nightclothes and slip into his bed. Their bed. The bed they should be sharing together.

"Your turn," Taylor said, jolting him back to earth.

He took a cold shower, trying to tell himself that a night on the hard floor would be good for his character.

But when he came out of the bathroom, the bed

was empty. He peered over it. Taylor lay in the sleeping bag, her eyes closed and her face relaxed.

This was wrong. Totally wrong. She'd come back to Montana at his request, to help him out, and she'd already gone way beyond the call of duty. He opened his mouth to tell her so, but she said, "Get over it, Jake. Get into bed and go to sleep."

She hadn't even opened her eyes.

"No, Taylor. This isn't right."

"Deal with it."

For some reason it seemed important to her, so he smothered his masculine pride and dealt with it. But he wasn't happy. He ran the towel through his hair one more time, shoved his fingers through it so it wouldn't be too much of a mess in the morning, and got into bed.

He missed her immediately. Having her in his bed, in his arms, had been a powerful sensation, had given him a deep sense of homecoming. All day he'd felt wonderful, and he knew his good mood had been because of his night with Taylor.

She made him happy, and it frightened him. It struck to the root of his fears, brought back all the unpleasant memories of vulnerability.

But if he didn't conquer those fears, if he didn't get over his past, he'd never have a chance at any kind of lasting happiness with anyone.

"Jake?"

He moved over to the side of the bed so he could look down at her. "Yes?"

"I'm glad everything's okay."

Her eyes still closed, she extended her hand up toward him. He stared at it in the dimness for a fraction of a second, not knowing what she wanted. Then he did the only sensible thing. He enfolded her hand in his own. He felt a slow-burning warmth at the touch, the kind of warmth and connection that burns for a long time to come, and he felt his body relax, as if the warmth from her hand was a smooth stroke across all his sore muscles, calming them, bringing relaxation so he could fall into a deep and restful sleep.

He lay on his side, his head pillowed on his free arm, the other draped over the side of the bed so he could maintain contact with his wife.

He listened to her breathing and felt the heat of her palm against his. Her breathing slowed, became deep and rhythmic. Her hand twitched in his, tightening suddenly a few times before coming to rest in a soft, relaxed curl around his own.

She was asleep, and when he woke up the next morning he was still holding her hand.

It was the kind of day that made everything worthwhile, that made Montana seem like paradise on earth, Jake thought, even in the middle of January.

Every remnant of the storm had vanished. The big sky above them was a glorious, uninterrupted blue, stretching from horizon to horizon with nothing to mar its brilliance.

The air was perfectly still. Smoke from the chimneys of the ranch buildings rose straight into the air, whirling and curling within their columns as hot air met cold.

Now that the sun was out they'd shut off most of the generators to conserve fuel. Only the low rumble of the one behind the calving barn reached Jake's ears as he stood on the porch sipping from a fresh cup of coffee. He saw two of his ranch hands chopping ice from the watering troughs in the winter pasture, and heard the occasional bellow of a cow as she celebrated the end of the storm.

Noisy footsteps interrupted his reverie. He stepped aside just in time to dodge two young hellions being chased out the door by his beautiful young wife.

Frankie and Billy leaped down the porch stairs and into the snowdrifts. They sank up to their waists, but this only made them shout louder and more happily as they floundered around, sending up clouds of snowflakes.

Taylor herself leaped into the snowbank beside them, landing on her back and swishing her arms and legs back and forth to make an angel in the snow. The two boys watched in fascination as an adult—a bona fide adult—descended to their own level of silliness.

Taylor's laughter rang out through the still morning. It gripped at something deep in Jake's heart, something he almost didn't want to acknowledge.

She taught the two Texan boys how to make snow angels. Soon the area in front of the house looked as if a whole troop of angels had come down to earth.

He didn't hear Hank behind him until the older

man cleared his throat. "Kinda surprising they can actually make snow angels. Snow devils is more their style, don't ya think?"

Jake laughed. "They're good kids, Hank. They've just got a little bit of extra energy."

"You can say that again. Darn kids run me ragged. Not that I don't love 'em."

Melissa came out on the porch dressed for the snow. Taylor waved her over. "I bet we can build a snow-being faster than Frankie and Billy can," she challenged.

Melissa grinned back at her. "No problem!" She slogged through the snow over to Taylor and immediately began packing up a big snowball for the base of their snow-being.

The boys looked on in surprise for a few seconds, and then with whoops of excitement began piling snow into a great big heap.

"Five bucks says my boys are going to win," Hank said.

"Ten says the women will do a better job."

Hank laughed. "That's a bet I'm not going to take."

Taylor shouted his name. "Hey, Jake!"

He looked over to find her grinning at him from behind the growing base of her snow-being.

"I bet we could beat the two of you, too!"

"How much do you want to bet, Taylor?"

The sparkle in her eye was the only answer.

"I could beat you alone, with one hand tied behind my back," he told her.

"Big words, Jake."

He put down his coffee mug and strode into the snow. She came running over and pulled his left arm up behind his back. "Go for it!" she challenged.

He laughed, bending down to start scooping snow. He was already off balance with his arm behind his back, and when Taylor bumped up against him he went sprawling into the snow.

"Look, everyone," he heard Taylor say, "Jake made a one-winged snow angel."

He sat up, brushing the snow from his face. "Taylor..." he said, caught between a growl and a laugh.

She grinned at him, totally unrepentant. "Sorry."

"No you aren't." He lunged for her, capturing her around the waist and bringing her down into the drift with a squeal. Holding her with the weight of his body, he scooped up a handful of snow and held it a foot over her face.

"Don't," she said. "Don't you dare."

He flexed his fingers just enough to dislodge a few little chunks of snow from the edge of the handful. One floated down to her cheek, the other landed on the bridge of her nose.

"Jake, so help me, if you—"

Jake looked down into her suddenly wide eyes, wondering why she'd broken off in the middle of her sentence.

Just then an immense load of snow hit the back of his head. Rolling sideways, he stared up at the mischievous face of Melissa, who held another load of snow at the ready.

"You're distracting my partner," the girl said. "Cut it out or face the consequences."

Taylor sat beside them, brushing snow out of her hair and laughing like a gleeful little girl. Jake shoveled his hand into the snow and flipped it all over Taylor. Immediately he got doused by Melissa.

It was all-out war. Even the boys put aside their snow-being long enough to join in. Jake felt like a kid. A thirty-six-year-old kid, playing in the snow.

When he finally disengaged himself he was soaked through to the skin and had never felt happier. He stumbled through the snow back to the porch, where Hank waited for him.

"Sure is nice to be in love," Hank said. "You and the little lady have something special. That's a fact."

It wasn't until he was inside on his way upstairs that the truth of Hank's words hit him full-force.

He was in love with Taylor. Completely, madly, head over heels in love with Taylor. He'd been in love with her the summer before, too, but this felt different. More real. More true.

And she would be leaving soon. In a few days Hank and the kids would be heading back home. Jake would have his new land and Taylor's presence wouldn't be necessary anymore. Hell, he'd promised to pay for their divorce when she got back to Boston. He would set her up in a new apartment, get her a better job and whatever clothes she needed to stay on her feet. Then he'd leave her to make her own way in the world.

He didn't kid himself. The new Taylor was a

fighter. In a few years he'd probably see her on the cover of *Business Week,* having shot up from waitress in a grubby downtown diner to CEO of a vast network of upscale restaurants.

She wasn't a spoiled brat anymore. She wasn't the woman he'd married. That should have made him happy. But it only made him feel like he'd just tangled with the sharp end of an angry bull.

Chapter Nine

Taylor was still racing to finish her snow-being when Jake came back out through the front door a few minutes later, dressed in dry work clothes. He approached her with an odd look on his face, but said only that he was going off to check on the ranch and he'd be back in a while.

When the kids tired of playing she got them inside and dried off, then joined Hank in front of the fire.

"You grew up in Boston, didn't you, Taylor?"

She nodded warily. Was it only her own guilty conscience that made the question seem pointed?

"Beautiful city, Boston. I was there once, about forty years ago. I bet it's changed a lot."

She nodded. It had certainly changed a lot in her mind, especially recently. Growing up in Boston she'd always felt as if it were *her* city. She'd lived in a safe neighborhood, had been able to enjoy all the delights the city could offer. She'd sailed in Boston harbor, gone to museums, spent part of every summer in Marblehead, or on the Cape, or the Vineyard or Nantucket. Usually with friends, granted, not her parents, but still...

Only in the past few months had she learned of the other side of the city, the part she'd always carefully locked her car doors against. She'd had to live among people who never could have dreamed of the advantages she'd had, people like Candy and the other waitresses at the Pancake Hut, who still approached life with an open spirit.

And coming back to the ranch she'd learned to see yet another side of Boston. Being here made her realize how limited and constrained even her prepoverty experience had been.

She'd thought herself hemmed in and imprisoned on the ranch with Jake last summer. But in Boston she'd been stuck in the narrow world of wealthy Bostonians, locked into an endless round of meaningless parties and empty social striving. Here, however, that wasn't the case. Oh, as Jake's wife she was still a wealthy woman compared to the hands who worked on the ranch, with freedoms they didn't share, but when animals were in jeopardy all the barriers fell away and everyone pulled together to help out.

"You ever get tempted to go back?"

She jerked her gaze over to Hank, who sat in front of the fire with his eyes closed in bliss. "Back to Boston?"

"Sure. Pick up and fly back for a little bit of excitement."

"I, uh, I like it here," she said, trying to be truthful without telling the whole truth.

Hank was silent for a minute. "Not everyone who comes out here makes it, Taylor. You're quite a gal, so you've got a good chance, but when you grow up in a city it's hard to make the adjustment." His eyes opened. "I was from the city myself, before I bought land out here and tried to become a rancher. Lasted almost thirty years, but after my wife died I couldn't handle the isolation anymore. Just goes to show that a strong relationship can get you through almost anything the world can throw at ya."

His words went straight to her heart. Her relationship hadn't been strong at all.

Hank relaxed back toward the fire, soaking up the warmth. "I knew Jake's mom," he said at last. "Pretty girl. Nothing compared to you, but pretty nonetheless. Couldn't handle life out here. Wanted to be back in the city where things were going on."

Taylor forced a laugh. "Things sure go on around here. These past few days, especially."

Hank shrugged. "Some people don't like it."

"Jake said she left when he was very young." That was all she knew about his mother. What had he yelled at her? *You lasted one month, Taylor. Even my mother lasted longer than that.*

She'd always been satisfied with the scant history Jake had sketched out for her during their all-too-brief courtship: his mother had left, he'd told her, and his father and grandfather had run the ranch together until he was old enough to take over.

Ever the stoic cowboy, Jake wouldn't be the kind to trot out a sob story about his deprived childhood.

Hank shook his head. "No one around here understood how she could leave a newborn like that."

"Newborn?" Taylor asked, incredulous. That was much worse than she'd thought.

Hank nodded. "Pretty shocking. Some of the local women wouldn't have minded becoming the second Mrs. Cassidy, but Jake's father never looked twice at them." Hank rocked back and forth for a moment, then added, "Don't think he could trust a woman not to leave him."

Hank put his hands on his knees and levered himself upright. "Well, I think I'd better go for a walk while I can still move. Haven't got many more miles left in these old bones, so I've got to make the best of them."

He walked out of the living room.

Taylor moved closer to the fire, feeling suddenly chilled. She put another log on it, then tried to build up a blaze that could drive the chill away.

Jake's mom had left him when he was a newborn. Rejected him before she even knew him.

No wonder he'd forged such a strong connection to his ranch that he valued it above real human intimacy. No wonder he'd spent more time working than he'd spent with his wife.

Taylor had thought marriage to Jake would help her escape the past. She'd wanted it to be totally unlike her parents' passionless marriage. But she'd un-knowingly revived *Jake's* past, and in painful detail. She'd been nothing more than an updated version of his mother. Just another city girl who couldn't handle life in Montana.

She thought of the words she'd flung at him the day she left. *If we'd ever talked, we might have had a chance.*

Brat that she was, she'd meant that if they'd talked more about *her* they might have had a chance. But if they'd talked more about him, she might have figured out what made him tick. They might have developed some real emotional closeness.

Was it too late?

She kept coming back to the same question. Was it too late? Could they have a second chance? Was there anything left to salvage?

And if there was, how could she be sure that salvaging it was the right thing to do?

Because if she stayed, it would have to be forever. She couldn't make a halfhearted commitment. She couldn't just *try* to make things work and have an easy out if they didn't.

She cared too much for Jake to put him through that kind of pain, to be the woman who ran out on him not once but twice.

Jake returned from his tour of the ranch and found Taylor working in the kitchen. Natural light streamed in through the windows, glinting off the polished chrome on the appliances and the glossy polished floor. She stood at the baking table with her hands covered in flour, a cookbook open in front of her and ingredients stacked on every side.

Her hair was loose, and there were little smudges of flour on her cheek and on her hair where she'd pushed it back.

"What are you doing?"

"Making bread."

"Making bread?"

"Yeah. It sounded like fun."

"Have you ever done it before?"

"Nope. Would you mind putting my hair up?"

"Barrette or headband?"

"Barrette. There's a couple upstairs in the bathroom or..." She hesitated. "Or there's one in my pocket."

In her pocket. Great.

"I'm not trying to seduce you, Jake. You can go upstairs if you want."

He sighed. She was going to be the death of him. "Which pocket?"

She pointed with her chin to the right front pocket of her faded blue jeans. Jake fished into her pocket, feeling the heat of her leg against the backs of his fingers. "Where's Irma?" he asked, trying to distract himself from the feel of her as he pulled out the barrette.

"I knew you were going to ask that." He could hear the grin in her voice. "I told her to go spend some time with her husband. The whole afternoon, in fact."

He put the barrette between his teeth and ran both hands through her hair. It slid wonderfully between his fingers, like a sexy seductive living thing. He collected it with exaggerated care. He combed her hair backward with his fingers, lingering over her scalp, and clipped it carefully into the barrette. "Who's cooking dinner?"

She looked up at him with wide, trusting eyes. "I thought we'd order a pizza."

"Order a pizza? From which universe? Even if the roads were clear, there's no pizza parlor until you get two towns down the road. This isn't—"

He broke off when she started laughing at him.

"This isn't Boston," he finished, feeling foolish. "So what are you making for dinner?"

"Me?" she said. "You'd trust me to cook dinner?" She shook her head. "Irma got everything ready. All I have to do is put it in the oven and warm it up."

He looked around at the almost-spotless kitchen. "I'd be lying if I said I wasn't relieved," he murmured.

"Careful, Jake..."

"That's right. You're the one with the lump of soggy dough in your hands."

"Not for long."

As Jake watched, she sprinkled flour over the dough and kneaded it on the breadboard. Her white button-down shirt—one of his, he realized—was rolled up to the elbows. He watched her bare forearms as she folded the dough toward her and pushed it down and away, again and again. "You do that well."

She grinned at him over her shoulder. "I watched someone do it on a cooking show once." She kneaded the dough for a few minutes, her eyes back on her task. "I think Hank suspects something."

His attention snapped away from sensual thoughts of her strong hands kneading the sore muscles of his back. "What makes you say that?"

"He asked me if I ever thought about going back to the city. He made a big point of how hard it is for city people to last out here."

"Damn."

"You think he's guessed?"

"I don't know. Maybe he's just being his usual tactless self."

"More like subtle as a fox. I don't know what to think."

"I don't, either. I just ran into him down by the barn and he said something about finishing up our business now that the storm has gone by. Can't figure why he'd say that if he knew our relationship was a fake."

She sprinkled more flour over the dough. "I thought we'd been doing a pretty good job."

"So did I, Taylor. So did I." He went to the kitchen table and sat on a painted wooden chair. There was a plate of madeleines on the table. He ate one, enjoying the way it melted in his mouth. "We couldn't have done any better. If he's guessed the

truth then we're at his mercy. Nothing to be done
about it.''

Taylor didn't answer, just kept working at her
bread. They fell into a companionable silence. She
watched her dough, and he watched her, enjoying the
sight of her muscles flexing on her bare forearms and
the way she rose up on her toes with every kneading
motion, lifting herself up so she could press down into
the dough with the weight of her body.

Taylor kneaded the dough for a few more minutes,
then stopped and pushed it into a big ball. She
reached for a bowl. ''How do you feel about kids,
Jake?''

Kids. The question was serious and calm, and it
took him a little bit by surprise. Taylor put the dough
into the bowl and covered it with a towel, then set it
inside the oven to rise. The Taylor he'd known last
summer hadn't asked him a lot of personal questions.
''Really? How do I really feel about kids?''

''Yeah,'' she said. She didn't meet his eyes, but
instead went to the sink and dampened a sponge to
start cleaning up the breadboard.

''I don't know,'' he confessed, surprised that the
truth came so easily. ''I think everyone wants the next
generation to take over for them, to carry on what
they've built up. But sometimes… Well, sometimes I
just don't know.''

He'd always wanted to have children and raise
them here on his ranch, but it had always seemed
horribly unfair to bring a child into the world not
knowing if its mother would desert it.

Taylor wiped the board down with smooth, precise movements, sweeping the flour into her cupped hand. Tossing the waste into the garbage, she came back to roll up the bag of flour and put away the jar of yeast and the other ingredients and utensils she'd used.

He followed her to the sink, leaning against the counter while she washed up. She hadn't reacted to his answer, except to look thoughtful and a little bit far away as she cleaned. "How about you?"

"I don't know, either." She gave him a sort of half smile, a little wavery around the edges. She wiped the measuring spoons and squeezed out the sponge. She rinsed the dishes and stacked them in the drain rack. "I used to want children like crazy. But I didn't have a clue what I would have been getting into." She laughed. "Can you imagine me as I was last summer having kids? What a disaster!"

He grinned along with her. She'd been too selfish to be a good parent back then, but after seeing her with Melissa, Frankie and Billy these past few days, he knew she had the makings of a good mother.

And a good rancher.

And a good lifetime partner.

Something fell into place. He'd always blamed her for being the first to give up on their marriage, for running away. But hadn't he given up on their marriage the moment they'd come to the ranch? Hadn't he run away from her, buried himself in work so he wouldn't have to face the emotional risk of being in love?

And wasn't that what had helped drive her back to Boston?

But what could he do about it now? Blurt out, "It's my fault our marriage ended and I want you back"?

Small steps. He had to take it in small steps. They had a lot of wounds to heal. A future together was a long way off.

He smiled at Taylor. "You're wonderful with those three kids," he told her, meaning it.

"Thanks. You know, my parents didn't give me a good model of how to raise a child. They spoiled me without loving me, and I never had them to depend on, to trust. But I feel as if I could do things differently. I feel as if I could provide the things a child would need."

She dried her hands on a kitchen towel, then took three loaf pans from a cupboard. After greasing them with butter, she set them aside and sat down at the kitchen table.

He joined her. "You'd make a good mother, Taylor."

Just then a loud thump sounded upstairs, followed by a crash and the sound of glass breaking.

They both jumped to their feet and dashed upstairs.

Frankie and Billy stood in their room, both in tears but unhurt. The floor lamp was at a crazy angle. The top poked through the window and cold air streamed into the room.

"We didn't mean to do it!" Frankie wailed. "It was an accident."

Taylor wrapped the younger boy in her arms. Billy

stood beside her. He wiped away his tears with his sleeve and sniffled his sobs to a halt, looking embarrassed to be caught crying.

Jake closed the door so the rest of the house wouldn't drop in temperature. "It's okay, guys. Things happen."

"What did happen?" Taylor asked, her voice gentle.

Frankie still sobbed against her. Billy said, "We were jumping back and forth between the beds. I bumped into Frankie and lost my balance and fell into the lamp. I'm really sorry."

"It's okay," Jake said again. "Why don't we all go downstairs to the living room and then I'll come back to clean up the glass."

Taylor carried Frankie downstairs and walked with a hand on Billy's shoulder, comforting him as much as he would let her. She settled the boys on the couch and sat with them, tucking her legs up underneath herself.

When Jake left the living room a few moments later, Taylor was telling the boys about a priceless vase she'd broken at a friend's house when she was a little girl. The soft murmur of her reassuring words stayed with him as he climbed the stairs.

She was so good with them. So patient, so soothing.

He wanted her to be the mother of his children.

Chapter Ten

The power came back on an hour later, just as Taylor divided her dough into the loaf pans. The generator was off, but she'd plugged in the radio so it would come on if the power did.

Jake came in a few minutes later. "Power's back up, in case you haven't noticed," he said with a grin.

"I noticed," she said. That grin of his worked on her in ways she didn't want to think about, except that she wanted to be here the next time the power came back on.

"What are the kids up to?"

"Reading. All three of them."

"Those two boys are reading?"

"Yeah. Shocking but true. How's the ranch doing?"

"More or less okay. The roads are clear again."

"All the way to town?"

"All the way. You want to go out tonight?"

She laughed. "With two boys and Melissa in tow? How about we stay here and celebrate getting through the storm?"

After dinner they all went into the living room. Jake sat on the floor with the boys and played Monopoly while Hank, awake after dinner for once, entertained them all with stories of his life on the ranch and some of his world travels after he'd left Montana. Melissa sat with Taylor, idly leafing through a rock-and-roll magazine, reading and listening at the same time.

They repeated the same ritual the next evening, after a fun day of exploring the ranch with the children. It almost felt as if they were a family, even though Hank was a crazy old cowboy and his grandkids were a handful of trouble.

This was the kind of thing she'd wished for as a child, Taylor thought. Someone to play games with her, to read to her, to tell her stories. Simple things people did when they actually cared for each other, even a little bit.

She relaxed on the love seat and soaked up the atmosphere. It didn't really matter that they weren't all related by blood; right now they were close enough to a family to make her feel all warm inside.

Weathering the recent storm had brought them together.

It had certainly brought her and Jake closer together.

Every once in a while as he played Monopoly he

glanced at her over the boys' heads, a soft, conspiratorial smile on his lips. His glances made the room even warmer than the fire did. She felt as if she'd earned his respect. She'd proved she'd changed from the brat she used to be.

Living in the dregs of Boston had been worth it. And her parents had been right to yank her out of her playgirl life-style. It was probably one of the few positive things they'd ever done for her. Maybe once this week was over she could reestablish contact with them. If she approached them as an adult, rather than as a spoiled child, maybe they could develop some kind of relationship.

She had self-respect now. She was the kind of person she would want to have as a friend, the kind others could depend on.

Someone *she* could depend on.

Maybe if she could do last summer all over again, she wouldn't be so desperately needy; she wouldn't see Jake's involvement with the ranch as a personal slight. She'd be her own person and meet Jake halfway.

And maybe he would actually want to spend more time with her. No one wanted to be around someone who couldn't stand on her own two feet.

There might be hope for them. That mythical second chance she'd been mulling over all week.

But Jake would have to want it, too, would have to be willing to love her, to do his part and stop pushing her away.

"Taylor?" Melissa asked her, tapping on her

shoulder. "Taylor, you aren't listening. Don't you think this guy's cute?"

Taylor glanced down at the glossy magazine page. The cute guy in question was a young rock star with long hair and a scrawny body, a sneering grin on his lips. He was kind of cute, in a childish way, but when Taylor looked up from the magazine and met Jake's eyes, all thoughts of any other man vanished. "He's okay," she said distractedly. "I've seen better."

Melissa made a scoffing sound. "You're married to better. Jake's a real babe. But for the rest of us poor mortals..."

Taylor laughed, breaking her gaze away to look at Melissa. "I hate to sound like such an adult, Melissa, but you need to be patient. You're a very attractive girl, and you'll find a babe of your own. But it's not what a guy looks like that counts. Same for you, too."

Melissa rolled her eyes. "Beauty is only skin deep. I know."

Taylor shrugged. "A relationship based on physical attraction is nothing compared to a real emotional bond. Sometimes it's hard to believe that, but it's true."

"You sound like my guidance counselor."

Taylor laughed. "Sorry. I'll stop preaching."

She looked over at Jake again. His head was down, his concentration on the board. "I owe *what?*" she heard him say.

"Six hundred dollars," Frankie said proudly. "I built two houses there so you owe me big bucks."

Jake sighed and handed over the colorful cash.

"You boys are going to bankrupt me," he said, hanging his head.

Taylor's heart constricted. In that moment she knew with total clarity what she wanted her future to bring. She glanced at Melissa and said, "I'll be right back. There's something I've got to do upstairs."

When everyone had taken themselves off to bed, Taylor stood with her husband on the front porch, just as they had before. Tonight lights shone out all over the ranch compound. A little wind had returned to blow gently over the snow-covered ground. The moon played hide-and-seek behind the spotty cloud cover.

Only a few of yesterday's snow angels had survived. The rest had been trampled. But the few that remained seemed even more angelic with the light of the moon etching their contours.

The two snow-beings—one large and haphazard, the other smaller and well-shaped—stood side by side in front of the house, looking out over the ranch just as she and Jake did.

She saw the dark shapes of horses moving over the snowy ground in the corral. One of them whinnied. The big paint, she suspected. He was a noisy, domineering horse, and she couldn't wait to settle him down later in the year.

Her breath caught on her throat. Thinking of the future here was getting to be an inescapable habit. Now she looked forward to a skillful battle of wills with the big horse. Looked forward to being an integral part of life on the ranch, a hardworking participant in the job of raising cattle and hay and training horses and dealing with all the other parts of this rugged Western life.

Just as she had before, she leaned against Jake. But tonight it felt more natural, and it was just as natural when she took his hand and led him back inside the house.

Upstairs she pushed him into the shower ahead of herself, and when it was her turn she took a long, luxurious shower and patted herself down with body powder before slipping into a silk camisole and tap pants.

She hung her damp towel on the back of the bathroom door and walked out into the room. Jake sat on the edge of the bed, dressed in boxers and a T-shirt. His gaze snapped to hers, then slid down her body, taking in the cream silk and lingering over her curves before cutting reluctantly away.

"My sleeping bag is gone."

"Oh?"

"Yeah."

She shrugged, going to the closet to put her clothes in the hamper. She made a show of peering around in search of the sleeping bag. "Maybe Irma took it away."

"Maybe," he said, not sounding convinced.

"I guess you'll have to sleep in the extra blankets, then."

Silence. Then, "The blankets are gone, too."

She looked at him, eyes wide. "Oh, my."

"Taylor..."

She pulled aside the covers and slipped into bed. She scooted over to the far side, sitting up against the headboard.

He just looked at her, not moving.

For the first time since she'd set her plan in motion an hour earlier, she wondered if she was doing the right thing. Her heart was beating like crazy. Her whole body felt flushed and hypersensitive.

The pull between them was strong. But it was different than the pull had been between them six months ago. It was lower, an insistent tugging rather than frantic attraction. It was a slow burn, a bed of coals glowing deep orange and sending out waves of silent, intense heat with hardly a drift of smoke.

"Come to bed, Jake." Her voice came out in a low pitch, like a rumbling purr. She wasn't trying to be outrageously seductive but she couldn't seem to help it.

"Taylor…"

"It's okay, Jake. I know what I'm doing."

"Do you?"

"This isn't about self-control, Jake."

"No, it's about stretching my sanity to the breaking point."

"We both feel that way. Come to bed."

Slowly he stood. His long, tall body was magnificent, glorious in its perfection. She could see past that, though, to the man inside the perfect shell. To the man who'd been abandoned by his mother and his wife, who had no reason to trust a woman to be there for him, to stay the course.

She felt the grip of fear on her heart as self-doubt came crashing back, telling her she couldn't be the woman who would turn that around. But she banished those feelings, concentrating instead on the image of Jake, such a strong, caring man, so suspicious of any love that came his way.

He settled onto the mattress. His weight made her tilt toward him. With his actions she felt a subtle change in the dynamic between them. She might have set up this seduction by hiding the sleeping bag and blankets, but she was no longer the one in control. She reveled in the freedom of it, welcoming him with her eyes.

He stretched out beside her, propped on one elbow so his face was close to hers. His long legs lay beside her own, radiating warmth. He brushed a strand of hair away from her face. His fingers traced the shape of her ear, moved down to drift across the sensitive skin of her neck. He stroked her forehead with the tips of two fingers, the touch electrifying her, drawing out her response. He trailed down her cheek and jaw, bringing her face into line with his.

Their gazes met. The coals glowed hotter, redder, and she felt it deep inside her. A tiny flame licked up, flared, and settled back down into the slow smooth glow.

"No regrets," Jake said. His voice was only a whisper, a dark, sultry, powerful whisper.

It wasn't a question, but she let her eyes answer it anyway. No regrets. Not now and not ever.

Jake cupped her hip. Effortlessly he slid her down

the bed, snug against him. She felt silk shift against her skin and knew she'd done the right thing. She stared up at him, at his face looming over hers, desire in his eyes and in every line of his beautiful face—more than desire if she wasn't mistaken.

She lay agonizingly still. The old Taylor would have reached up to draw Jake's mouth down to hers. The new Taylor wasn't going anywhere. She waited and drowned in the feelings of anticipation, in the mad pounding of her heart as she lay beneath him.

And then he kissed her. Lightly. Tenderly. Reverently. It was as if he was kissing her for the first time. His hand against the small of her back pulled her against him, close to him, and his lips explored hers, tasting and sounding out the textures and the strength of her desire. She felt him against her thigh, more than ready. The contrast between that insistent part of him and the tenderness of his exploring lips made her melt inside, made her want this to last forever.

Jake touched her as if she were an angel fallen from heaven, as if by stroking her skin he could touch the core of her. She touched him, too, exploring everything, remembering the raging passion that had flared between them in the summer, but also feeling a host of new feelings. New sensations.

She touched all the hidden parts of him she'd just learned how to see. All the things she'd ignored the summer before, that she'd been too blind to see. His own needs. His own desire to be cared for, to be acknowledged and to be...loved. Unconditionally. Without reference to whether he spent enough time with her or always took care of her in the precise way she demanded.

Touching him this way she felt married, connected. She felt wonderful. As each new sensation washed over her it felt as if it was the only thing in her world, all she knew.

Nothing in her experience prepared her for the way she felt tonight in Jake's arms. She'd thought their lovemaking had been glorious the past summer, but she'd been wrong. This was truly glorious. This was the feeling she'd craved. Of being totally one with her husband. Of being able to reach out with her emotions as much as her hands.

All those nights she'd spent in her cold apartment dreaming of what had been, when she should have been dreaming about this. Dreaming about this feeling of homecoming, of everything being ecstatically right in the world.

And when Jake finally slipped inside her, claiming her as his wife, his mate, the homecoming was complete. Total. She surrendered everything to him and felt him surrendering everything to her, and she was happier than she ever could have believed possible.

Repleteness washed over her. She lay beneath her husband, his weight a pleasing reminder of the passion they had just shared. Her arms were snug around his back, pulling him down on top of her.

Five minutes had passed, and still neither one had spoken. Neither one could speak. Taylor's breathing was just returning to normal; Jake's was still ragged.

His eyes shone with a fierce passion for her; she couldn't look away.

"Taylor," he said at last, his voice low and rough, like the finest aged whiskey. She responded to the awe in his voice with a little shiver. "Taylor, I don't know what to say."

She smiled up at him. "I didn't know it could be like that, either."

"Incredible."

"I know."

"I thought we were good together. I thought…"

"I know." She felt giddy. "I know." She stroked his face, feeling the slight dampness in the tiny hairs at his temples. "I think we were meant to be together."

"Mmm."

She rolled out from underneath him and slipped into the bathroom, then came back out and collected her discarded silks. Unselfconscious, she first pulled on the tap pants and then slid into the camisole.

Knowing he watched her, she went over to the door and put her hand on the knob.

"Where are you going?" Jake asked lazily, still lying there on the bed.

"To get the sleeping bag," she said, smiling with mischief. "I put it in the linen closet."

Jake was out of bed in an instant, totally uninhibited as he crossed the room in two powerful strides and scooped her up in his arms. She squealed, but he didn't let her go. In seconds she was flat on her back on the bed, her camisole already pushed up above her breasts and her tap pants mysteriously down around her ankles. It was like the summer before, but better. Rawly sexual, but also connected on a deep and intense level.

Afterward Jake pulled back the curtains and they lay in each other's arms with moonlight washing over them.

Taylor savored the sensations of being back with Jake, being where she belonged. She didn't want to sleep, didn't want to lose this exquisite moment, but her eyes slowly closed and she drifted off, only to wake again a few moments later to find Jake watching her with an expression of wonder on his face that made her stomach clench and her dreams of the future seem like they might come true.

Their closeness and connection was a miracle. A week ago she would have laughed if someone had suggested she would feel this way tonight, but somehow things had changed.

She knew it was in part because of her new openness toward Jake. She wanted to know more about him, to build on her understanding so that every time they came together it would be with more knowledge and more trust.

She bit her lip, then said, "Jake, can I ask you a question?"

Slow silence, the pause of a man who's experienced too much pleasure in too short a time to respond quickly to anything. "Sure. Ask me anything."

"What are you scared of, Jake?"

"Hmm?"

"Before the storm hit you told the boys you get scared sometimes. What do you get scared of?"

Another long pause. "That was just something I said."

"I know that. But I also know it was true." She grinned up at him. "Everyone gets scared, even big strong cowboys like you."

"Taylor, what brought this on?"

"I'm curious. That's all. You want to know what I'm scared of?"

"Sure."

She paused, thinking. "I'm scared of hurricanes, earthquakes and tornadoes. Of big ugly spiders and dogs with teeth that have been filed to sharp points. Hate groups, traffic accidents, and global warming. My boss. I used to be afraid of nuclear annihilation, but now I'm just afraid there'll never be another movie like *Philadelphia*."

She swallowed, knowing she was babbling. She couldn't stop herself from continuing. "I'm afraid to be alone. I'm afraid I'm unlovable." She felt a tear gather in each of her eyes, and hiccuped back the urge to cry. Her parents' emotional desertion still hit her hard. No wonder she hadn't been able to handle Jake's distancing last summer. "Dammit. I'm supposed to be asking you the questions, but you've got me all turned around."

"I feel the same way, Taylor."

She tried to smile. "You're afraid of earthquakes, too?"

"I'm all turned around, too."

He didn't say anything more.

The air filled with sudden tension, and Taylor regretted asking the questions she had. Regretted opening herself up. She didn't regret their lovemaking, but she knew she shouldn't have pushed things so quickly. Somehow the past few minutes had undermined the closeness she'd thought had developed.

She didn't even know what she'd hoped for. Was it for Jake to admit that he wanted her to stay? That he was afraid of being without her?

Or was it for him to say that he was afraid she would leave again, so that she could tell him she didn't want to?

Jake left her with a warm kiss before dawn, but she couldn't get back to sleep.

How could she sleep when last night had left her feeling as if nothing had changed, as if there was still a chasm between them?

She got out of bed and washed her face, staring at herself long and hard in the mirror, wondering what she should do.

She dressed and went over to the closet, where she pulled out her suitcase and fished in the inner pocket for the travel documents she'd gotten in Boston. She opened the envelope and unfolded the itinerary. Her return flight was for tomorrow, though it was an open fare and she could travel whenever she wanted without a penalty.

Tomorrow. That was when they'd expected to be through with each other. That was when she'd planned to be so desperate to leave the ranch that she would leap into a truck and beg to be driven to the airport so she could fly back to her horrible apartment and her horrible job and her horrible lonely life in Boston. Now she didn't know what to think.

She flipped to the ticket coupon and held it in her hands. Twelve hours earlier she'd been convinced she'd never use the ticket, that she would do whatever it took to stay here. She wasn't so sure anymore. If Jake were willing to meet her halfway, to do his part to make their marriage work, wouldn't he have found a way to let her know?

The bedroom door opened just then, and Jake stepped into the room. He grinned at her, saying, "I couldn't resist coming back to say good morning again," but then his gaze landed on the suitcase and on the open itinerary and his smile faded.

Taylor didn't move, didn't speak. There was nothing she could say—no quick denial, but no declaration that she was leaving him, either. They held each other's gazes for a long moment, but Jake's eyes were cold and closed off, and there was no communication.

Say something, she urged him silently. *Tell me how you feel.*

But he didn't.

Jake turned, and a fraction of a second later he was gone, the door shutting softly behind him.

Tears welled in Taylor's eyes. She knew she had to leave. They couldn't have a marriage if only one of them was willing to make it work.

Chapter Eleven

She was leaving him.

Jake stood in the open door of the calving shed, looking out over his land. Normally the wide sweep of country would have soothed him, but today he saw only the vast emptiness of it.

It echoed the hollow feeling inside of him. The all-too-familiar hollow feeling.

Taylor was leaving him again.

Despite everything they'd shared in the past week, despite the progress he thought they'd made, she couldn't wait to go.

Maybe she'd lied last night. Maybe their lovemaking hadn't been as amazing for her as it had been for him. Maybe she'd only seduced him for the hell of it.

He shook his head in disgust. He was such a fool. Such a sucker.

A thousand tasks around the ranch demanded his attention, but today he didn't care. Today he couldn't do anything but stand here wallowing in the insanity of this situation.

He'd thought he could handle it. He'd thought it wouldn't matter to have Taylor back on the ranch, back in his house, back in his bed. He'd thought he was over her.

He hadn't even begun to get over her.

He was as in love with her as he'd been when he married her. More so.

Dammit, he didn't want her to go. He wanted her to stay here. To live with him. To work beside him on the ranch.

He'd give up everything to make that happen.

He would do anything to keep her.

The realization floored him. He took a deep breath, and as the cold winter air filled his lungs he felt the tension leave his body. The hollow, aching feeling disappeared.

Since the moment he'd married Taylor, he'd been running from her, pushing her away. Well, that wasn't going to happen any longer.

He didn't know how, but everything was going to work out. He'd make sure it did.

After breakfast Hank shooed his grandkids away, saying he wanted to talk business with Jake and Taylor.

An alarm bell went off in Taylor's mind. The land deal was supposed to be between Hank and Jake. She didn't want to be part of it, not now that she knew she wouldn't be staying. But Hank patted the chair beside his, and she saw she had no choice but to participate.

Hank riffled through a folder of documents in front of him. "I sure ain't sorry to be getting rid of this land," he said. "It's been good to me, but I'm too old to mess around with Montana winters."

He fixed Jake with a look. "As you know, there's been a couple of other offers, but I've got my reasons for wanting to sell it to you. You've got history in this area, and you've got a nice family operation going. I don't want my land chopped up into pieces and sold to wannabe cowboys from Los Angeles or New York. Call me a sentimental old fool, but I want to see the ranching way of life live on. I've thought long and hard about this decision, and that's why I wanted to come by one last time to make sure the land was going to the right people."

She'd expected Jake to look uncomfortable when Hank talked about a "nice family operation," but he didn't.

"It's got to go to people with a sense of permanence," Hank continued. "People who can be stewards of the land for another generation. Not some corporate rancher who's gonna overgraze to take quick profits and leave the land in ruin. No, sir."

He looked fondly over at Taylor. "You all haven't started the next generation yet, but you will, and I know you'll try to make this little part of the earth safe and secure for your children."

She had a difficult time keeping a pleasant smile on her face. Hank's words were hard to take. She felt hurt and exposed, and foolish for thinking she could have had a future here.

"I've seen how the two of you take care of things. The people who work for you are happy, and the animals get good care. Maybe it seems like a silly thing, but it makes an old man happy to know that my land's going to people who value it."

"Thanks, Hank," Jake said, his expression betraying nothing but appreciation for what Hank had just said. It was as if he hadn't seen her with the ticket in her hands, didn't know their marriage was ending again.

Hank plucked a pen from his pocket and said, "All right. Enough rambling. As I told you, I knocked a few thousand off the price for the inconvenience of our unexpected visit, and also because it's going to cost some money to bring that cabin back into shape. No arguments, all right? Taylor, you come on over here and sign this first, then we'll let Jake do his John Hancock."

Taylor glanced at the document, which transferred the property to both herself and Jake. Not at all what she'd expected when she'd agreed to come to Montana.

Well, they'd get a lawyer to straighten it out later. Right now her job was to sign the paper.

She signed, feeling like a fraud.

She pushed the contract toward Jake. He signed with a flourish, looking pleased with himself.

He'd obviously gotten over his momentary anger at seeing her with the airline ticket. His pride had been injured. But now he had the land, and he was rid of her. Everything he'd always wanted.

Knowing that didn't make the thought of leaving any easier.

Late that morning while Jake packed the car for Hank and the kids, Hank pulled Taylor aside. "He's a good man. You two will be able to make it."

Be able to make it? The remark took her by surprise. "Er, of course we will, Hank." She hated the lie, hated the way the truth ripped her up inside.

He smiled back at her, his face kindly and understanding. "You don't have to pull the wool over my eyes anymore, Taylor. I know you all have been having trouble. But I'm sure things are going to work out."

She watched Hank for a long moment. The man was definitely sharper than she'd given him credit for, and there was no point in playing innocent. "How…how did you find out?"

Hank shrugged. "Things just didn't add up. Jake was pretty weird about ya when I first talked to him on the phone. Seemed to be making up answers when I asked after your health. Then when I showed up here you guys were all over each other like a couple of newlyweds. That kind of see-mented my suspicions, but it wasn't until I overheard one of the hands saying something about how much you'd changed since you left that I figured out how bad things had gotten.''

She felt stricken. ''Hank, I'm so sorry we tried to deceive you. We shouldn't have done it.''

He winked at her. ''Well, now I'm not so sure about that. Got ya back together, didn't it? Heck, may not have been the most honest thing you both ever did, but a lasting marriage is a pretty good reward, I say.''

Her stomach hurt. ''Hank, nothing's been finalized. We don't know what's going to happen.''

He put his hand on her shoulder. ''I bet things are better than you think. Jake may look like a tough cowboy on the outside, but he's got a soft spot a mile wide on the inside.'' He picked up his two suitcases. ''You invite me to the christening, okay?''

She didn't know what to say. ''A little soon for plans like that, don't you think?''

He winked at her. ''Y'all are in love. It'll happen eventually.'' He went down the steps and into the waiting vehicle.

Taylor and Jake stood on the porch together, waving at Hank and the kids as they drove off down the snowy drive.

When the car was finally out of sight, Jake dusted off his hands and turned to smile at Taylor. ''Thank you.''

She couldn't manage to smile back. ''You got what you wanted,'' she said. ''Congratulations.''

''Not quite.''

She turned away. "Right. Don't worry about that, Jake. I'll sell you my half for a dollar."

"It's worth more than that."

Why did his voice have to sound so sexy, so self-possessed? "I'm wiped out, Jake. I'm going upstairs."

He looked as if he wanted to say something, but didn't. She went inside and climbed the steps. Jake headed for his office.

In his bedroom—she'd started thinking of it as *his* again—she looked at the bed and realized she couldn't handle another night here. She had to get away, even if it meant spending the night in a motel.

She pulled her suitcase out of the closet and began packing. In the bathroom she collected her shampoo and conditioner, her face powder and mascara. She placed them carefully in her toiletry kit.

Irma had done laundry the night before, so most of her clothes were neatly put away in the drawers. She packed neatly and methodically, not hurrying but not dawdling, either.

She'd finished the top drawer when she looked up and saw Jake. He lounged in the doorway, watching her with a wry smile on his lips.

She kept packing. She remembered the way she'd hurled her belongings into her suitcase five months ago, the way Jake had looked at her with unamused condescension.

His attitude now was hard for her to understand.

"I'm leaving, Jake." She said the words in a calm, matter-of-fact tone. She'd rehearsed them in her head.

No response. She folded a shirt and laid it on top of the others in the suitcase.

"I noticed," he said at last.

"I can't stay." She picked up her nightshirt. "Not like this."

"Of course not." He waved a hand at the nightshirt. "May I have that?"

The question startled her. She looked down at the soft, faded fabric of the Cassidy's Dry Goods T-shirt. "This?"

"Yeah."

It was his, after all, even though he'd said it looked better on her. "Sure."

He straightened and closed the distance between them with that animal grace he'd always possessed.

She handed him the shirt and immediately felt bereft. It didn't matter that leaving him was the right thing to do, the only thing to do. Her love for him wasn't going to disappear overnight.

Jake tucked the collar of the shirt under his chin and folded the shirt against his chest. He carried it to the top dresser drawer she'd emptied a moment before and set it down inside.

When he moved out of the way, Taylor pushed in the top drawer and opened the next one down. Picking up two pairs of pants, she turned to go back to the dresser.

Jake stood by the suitcase, one of her new shirts in his hands.

"You want that one, too?" she asked.

"Yeah."

"Take it. You paid for it, after all."

"Thanks." He moved toward the dresser. "But that's not why I want it."

She tossed the two pairs of pants into the suitcase, not caring that they got a little wrinkled. Again she had to push the top dresser drawer closed to get to more of her things. When she turned, Jake stood over her suitcase, riffling through her clothes. "What are you doing?"

Unperturbed by her question, he selected a few items, including one of the pairs of pants she'd just packed, as well as her peach silk camisole. He put the clothes in the top drawer and went back for another load. "Do you remember what you said the other night about your fears?"

"Remind me."

"You said you're afraid you're unlovable."

She feigned nonchalance. "So?"

"You're not."

Coming from him…well, that didn't mean much. "Thanks. That's obviously why you're so glad to get rid of me."

He ignored her sarcasm and self-pity. "I'm afraid of things, too."

She didn't say anything.

"A lot of things." He grinned at her out of the side of his mouth. "Even a big strong cowboy like me."

That grin. She wouldn't let it work on her. "What are you afraid of?" The question was cool. She didn't want him to get to her. Anyway, she'd asked him this before.

There was silence for so long she thought he'd forgotten the question.

"I'm afraid of losing you."

She stopped in her tracks. "Excuse me?"

He also stopped. They each held an item of clothing. "I'm afraid of losing you. Very, very afraid."

She sat down on the edge of the bed. "Jake..."

He took the shirt out of her hands and placed it on the bed. He sat next to her. "There's one thing I'm not afraid of, though. Not anymore. I used to be afraid of it. I used to run from it. I even ran from it this morning, before I came to my senses."

He took her hand in his. "I know you want to leave me, Taylor. I haven't been the kind of man you need, the kind you deserve. I've been pushing you away, protecting myself, since the day we met. I was afraid you would leave me, but I didn't realize my attitude toward you would drive you away."

"It did."

"I'll always be afraid of losing you, Taylor, but I'm not afraid to love you." He squeezed her hand in both of his. "I want you to stay. I want you to be my partner, to be the impetuous debutante I fell in love with last summer and the hardworking rancher I fell more deeply in love with this past week. I want you to work beside me. I want you to live with me and share my life. I need you to stay."

She didn't know how to respond. Her life had shifted abruptly again. Everything she wanted was within her grasp, but she couldn't seem to remember how to speak.

Jake slipped off the bed and got down on his knees. "Taylor, I love you. I'm begging you to stay."

She felt a tear form in each eye. They ran down her cheeks. She opened her mouth, meaning to say, "Yes, I'll stay," but instead she hiccuped back a sob and said, "Free room and board?"

It was a crazy thing to say, and they both knew it. Jake laughed, love shining in his eyes. "Please stay."

She gave him a watery smile. She got off the bed, too, and came down to his level. She wrapped her arms around his neck. "Yes, Jake. I'll stay forever."

He looked down into her eyes. "Welcome home."

Epilogue

"Okay, I'll tell them. Bye, Mom... I love you, too."

Taylor smiled as she hung up the phone on the wall in the kitchen. Her six-year-old daughter, Faith, stirred blueberries into the batter for their Sunday morning pancake breakfast. Charlie, who would turn four in a month, sat at the table drawing a picture of the barn with a purple crayon. "Grandma says hi and sends you both a big kiss."

"When are she and Grandpa coming to visit again?" Faith asked.

"Soon, I hope," Taylor said. In the past seven years she and her parents had grown a lot closer than before. It had been hard at first, but Jake had encouraged her to keep trying. It had been worth it. Though they'd all had to go through some painful, challenging times, her parents had gradually learned to be more caring and loving. They even seemed to be more loving with each other these days.

Taylor plucked the mixing bowl out of Faith's hands. She poured spoonfuls of batter onto the griddle. "Charlie," she said without turning around, "please call your father in for breakfast."

"He's already here," Jake said. He leaned against the door frame, surveying the idyllic scene before him. His family. The one he thought he'd never have.

Taylor turned to meet his eyes, a welcoming smile on her lips.

Those lips.

Those wonderful, kissable lips. As usual, he couldn't resist. He crossed the room in two easy strides and took his wife in his arms. "Hello, Taylor."

She leaned into his embrace. "Hello, Jake."

And then he kissed her, and it felt as wonderful as it had the very first time.

*   *   *   *   *

SOMETIMES BIG SURPRISES COME IN SMALL PACKAGES!

Celebrate the happiness that only a baby can bring in **Bundles of Joy** by Silhouette Romance!

February 1998
On Baby Patrol by Sharon De Vita (SR#1276)
Bachelor cop Michael Sullivan pledged to protect his best friend's pregnant widow, Joanna Grace. Would his secret promise spark a vow to love, honor and cherish? Don't miss this exciting launch of Sharon's *Lullabies and Love* miniseries!

April 1998
Boot Scootin' Secret Baby by Natalie Patrick (SR#1289)
Cowboy Jacob Goodacre discovered his estranged wife, Alyssa, had secretly given birth to his daughter. Could a toddler with a fondness for her daddy's cowboy boots keep her parents' hearts roped together?

June 1998
Man, Wife and Little Wonder by Robin Nicholas (SR#1301)
Reformed bad boy Johnny Tremont would keep his orphaned niece at any price. But could a marriage in name only to pretty Grace Marie Green lead to the love of a lifetime?

And be sure to look for additional BUNDLES OF JOY titles
in the months to come.

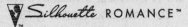

Find us at your favorite retail outlet.

MARIE FERRARELLA's

miniseries continues with her
brand-new Silhouette single title

In The Family Way

Dr. Rafe Saldana was Bedford's most popular pediatrician. And though the handsome doctor had a whole lot of love for his tiny patients, his heart wasn't open for business with women. At least, not until single mother Dana Morrow walked into his life. But Dana was about to become the newest member of the Baby of the Month Club. Was the dashing doctor ready to play daddy to her baby-to-be?

Available June 1998.

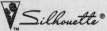

Find this new title by Marie Ferrarella
at your favorite retail outlet.

Look us up on-line at: http://www.romance.net   PSMFIFWAY

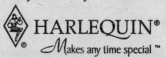

The World's Most Eligible Bachelors are about
to be named! And Silhouette Books brings
them to you in an all-new, original series....

World's Most
Eligible Bachelors

Twelve of the sexiest, most sought-after men share
every intimate detail of their lives in twelve never-
before-published novels by the genre's top authors.

Don't miss these unforgettable stories by:

Dixie Browning

Marie Ferrarella

Jackie Merritt

Tracy Sinclair

BJ James

RACHEL LEE

Suzanne Carey

Gina Wilkins

VICTORIA PADE

MAGGIE SHAYNE

Anne McAllister

Susan Mallery

Look for one new book each month in the
World's Most Eligible Bachelors series beginning
September 1998 from Silhouette Books.

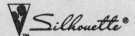

Silhouette ®

Available at your favorite retail outlet.

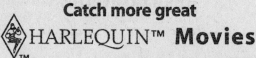

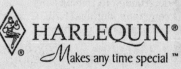

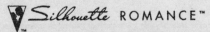